UPSTAIRS, DOWNSTAIRS

Rumours are flying around the servants' quarters at Brackenfold Hall. Items are going missing, and nobody knows who to trust anymore. Fingers start pointing at Bess, the sullen new scullery maid — but housemaid Sally Halfpenny feels sure she isn't to blame. Sally vows to uncover the true identity of the thief. Meanwhile, a fever has hit the whole village, and she fears for the safety of her parents. Not to mention the anguish of her unrequited love for footman James Armstrong . . .

ALICE ELLIOTT

◆

UPSTAIRS, DOWNSTAIRS

Complete and Unabridged

LINFORD
Leicester

First published in Great Britain in 2020

First Linford Edition
published 2021

A catalogue record for this book is available
from the British Library.

ISBN 978–1–4448–4802–1

Published by
Ulverscroft Limited
Anstey, Leicestershire

Printed and bound in Great Britain by
TJ Books Ltd., Padstow, Cornwall

This book is printed on acid-free paper

The servants' quarters of Brackenfold Hall buzzed with the patter of running feet and a whirlwind of panic rushed up and down the stairs.

A nasty strain of fever had hit the whole household and the result was absolute chaos. The members of staff who'd managed to escape the infection so far were having to cope the work of those who'd had no choice but to take to their beds.

Housemaid Sally Halfpenny felt the muscles in her back contract as she lugged the heavy bucket of cold compresses along the corridor towards the staircase up to the attic.

'I almost wish I had the fever, too,' Bess, the scullery maid, muttered as she walked behind Sally with a bowl of warm broth. 'I could do with the time off work.'

'Bess Trimble!' Sally set her bucket down for a moment and turned towards the younger girl.

'Have you seen poor Clare? She's thrashing around in her bed like nothing I've ever seen before and her forehead feels like a bonfire. Don't ever say anything like that again and especially not in front of her, even once she's better.'

'S'pose,' Bess replied as they carried on trudging along the corridor and then slowly made their way up the narrow stairs to the servants' bedrooms in the attic.

Clare was another of the housemaids and had fallen ill only the previous day. Julian Fairclough, the son of the wealthy clothiers who owned the Hall, was poorly, too.

His wife, Grace, and their two-year-old daughter, Florence, had fled to her parents' house further down the valley and over the border in Rochdale, as had the older Mr and Mrs Fairclough and their daughter, Amelia.

Nancy, Miss Amelia's lady's maid, had gone with the family, along with a few other servants.

'Hello, lovey,' Sally tried to keep her

voice bright as they entered Clare's room. Sally normally shared this bedroom with Clare but had temporarily moved in with Bess.

She instinctively raised a pocket handkerchief to her face in an attempt to avoid any infection. Her mother had given her a little bottle of lavender water the previous Christmas and she'd dabbed a few spots of it on the cotton, in the hope that the pleasant floral smell would ward off any bad germs.

Its soothing scent reminded Sally of her mother and she felt a sudden longing for their family cottage in Brackenfold village. Still, there was no time for sentiment now.

Clare had barely replied. Her lips were pale but her cheeks were flushed. She was normally such a cheery soul and it saddened Sally to see her like this.

'Come now and take just a little soup. It'll make you feel better.' Sally helped Clare sit up whilst Bess hovered by the door.

'I'll get back to the scullery,' Sally said

uncertainly. Nursing clearly didn't come very easily to her.

'Pop a pillow outside the bottom of the door on your way out,' Sally advised as Bess went to leave. 'We don't want the infected air escaping through the draught.'

Once Sally had coaxed Clare into taking as much soup as possible and laid a cold compress on her forehead, she quietly left the room and made her way out, making sure to position the pillow properly as she did so.

She left the bucket in the room so Clare could replace the compress any time she wanted, providing she stayed awake.

Sally would have gladly sat with her all day but there was an overwhelming amount of work to be done in the rest of the house and she couldn't stay in the attic long.

The rugs in the family bedrooms all needed shaking out, as did the curtains. The grates in the fireplaces hadn't been cleaned yet, either, and new coal was to be laid. It wouldn't do to have a cold house, especially with all the infections flying around.

It was a cold and icy February and there was no sign of winter relenting just yet.

Sally lost no time in hurrying along the polished wooden corridors of the first floor of Brackenfold Hall. Fairclough family portraits adorned the walls as well as pleasant rural scenes featuring water-wheels, haymakers and livestock grazing.

Of course, just like the rest of West Yorkshire, Brackenfold was an industrial place now, packed full of busy textile mills. Their tall smoking chimneys dom-inated the hills and valleys, transforming the small Pennine dwellings into impor-tant producers of cloth and carpets.

The largest of them was owned by Sal-ly's employer, Mr Victor Fairclough, and would eventually be inherited by Julian, his son, who'd already taken over most of the day-to-day running of the mill.

'Oh, there you are, Sally, thank good-ness.' Mrs Hartley, the housekeeper, was striding along the corridor at an even faster pace. 'We need your help. James came down with the fever this morning, poor lad. He's confined to his bed now.'

'Oh, no!' Sally cried, feeling her stomach contract in a nervous lurch. Of all the staff in the Hall, James Armstrong, the footman, was the last person she wanted taking ill.

Solid and dependable, he'd been a great source of support to both Mrs Hartley and Mr Sykes, the butler, throughout this crisis so far. The infection was spreading as fast as a moorland fire in a dry summer.

'Absolute disaster. I've had to call Dr Marshall again,' Mrs Hartley muttered. Her rounded face, which was normally so composed was now a worrying shade of mottled red and her mouth was screwed up in panic.

'Look, the rest of family are safe, so that's something.' Sally tried to keep her voice level, in the thin hope of reassuring the housekeeper, though she knew she'd never match the strength of James. Mrs

Hartley loved him like a son.

'And we're lucky the master has enough money to pay Dr Marshall to see to everyone. This new vapour oil he's been giving his patients is supposed to work like magic. Better times are ahead, I'm sure of it.'

Sally hoped she sounded more confident than she felt inside. Her worries were escalating to the folk in the village now, too. She felt particularly scared for her parents and brother, though of course a visit to them was impossible at the moment. There was too much work to be done at the Hall, and anyway, the risk of passing on the infection was far too high. Isolation was essential for now.

'I know, I know,' Mrs Hartley replied. She appeared to have taken Sally's words at face value. 'You'll need to include James on your list of patients. He'll require compresses and a bowl of broth, like Clare. Off you go.'

'Don't you want to look after him yourself?' Sally felt her stomach contract again and was acutely aware that her face was colouring with a deep red blush. Mrs Hartley, however, was oblivious.

'I have to see to Mr Julian now,' she replied shortly as she turned to leave. 'I'll go up and have a chat to James later,' she added, slightly more gently.

'We're in the middle of the worst fever Brackenfold has seen for years, Sally, and normal rules don't apply. Be a dear, won't you, and look after him. I'm sure Bess will help you. Your other duties will have to wait for now.'

'Of course, Mrs Hartley,' Sally answered dutifully as she went down to the kitchen in search of more broth.

Sally's heart was thumping in her chest as she made her way there. The Hall felt empty and the silence was eerie. She had never known the place to be so quiet.

It didn't take her long to reach the kitchen, where Mrs Ackroyd, the cook, stood scowling over a big copper pot.

'Ridiculous,' she muttered on seeing Sally appear in the doorway.

'Hello to you, too,' Sally answered

goodnaturedly, pushing her broken spirit and worries for James to one side. She knew by now that it was pointless to take offence at the cook's grumpy manner. She was like this with everyone.

Mrs Ackroyd had a moon-shaped face, piggy eyes and a ruddy complexion. Her thin lips were generally set in a gurn. Some of the younger maids were quite frightened of her, but Sally had been around long enough to take Mrs Ackroyd in her stride.

'I'm thoroughly sick of all this,' Mrs Ackroyd went on. She was using her wooden spoon to jab at the broth rather than stir it. 'I'm cooking broth by the gallon with no-one to help me. Ellie took to her bed this morning, too. She only made it till seven o'clock.'

'Oh, no!' Sally replied. She knew Mrs Ackroyd didn't like cooking for the other servants, preferring to focus solely on food for the Fairclough family themselves. Ellie, the kitchen maid, generally prepared the servants' meals.

'So, I'm stuck with this one for now,'

Mrs Ackroyd rolled her eyes as a sullen faced Bess emerged from the scullery and made her way to the chopping board on the kitchen surface. Several carrots and a few onions were sitting there waiting to be prepared.

Sally tilted her head to one side and gave the cook a disapproving look. It was somewhat reminiscent of how her mother would glare at Sally and her brother, William, whenever they misbehaved as children, though not quite as fierce. After all, Mrs Ackroyd was by far her superior in the servants' pecking order and Sally wasn't daft enough to push her luck.

Sally decided it wasn't worth upsetting the cook any further by asking for Bess's help again and, as she struggled back up the stairs with a bucket of compresses in one hand and a bowl of broth in the other, Sally distracted herself from her worries about James by turning her thoughts to the scullery maid.

She couldn't help but think that the rest of the staff were unnecessarily harsh on Bess. She'd noticed that, despite being something of a misery with everybody, Mrs Ackroyd was particularly rude to the scullery maid and the other servants weren't a whole lot better. She'd heard Ellie tutting under her breath about Bess, too, and even Clare, who was generally very kind-hearted, couldn't find anything nice to say about her.

'She doesn't exactly help herself much,' Clare had remarked to Sally one night as they prepared for bed, not long before she'd taken ill. 'She's always so sour-faced and never shows any enthusiasm for anything. I don't think I've ever once seen her smile.'

'I don't know,' Sally responded. 'She's found it hard to settle in here and perhaps her face naturally looks a bit dour. I'm sure she's not such a bad lass deep down.'

'You're more generous than me, our Sal,' Clare responded as she blew out the candle. 'You've never owt bad to say about anybody.'

Sally felt her eyes well up as she

thought back to the tortuous fever her good friend was facing now and the look of anguish in her eyes when she'd popped by to see her that afternoon.

She prayed Clare would feel better soon. She was missing their chats already. More than anything, Sally wished she could share her apprehensions about visiting James's bedside with someone who would understand.

She was nearing his bedroom now and could feel her nerves as they raced round her body in a frenzy.

Sally's hands were too full to knock on James's bedroom door so she tapped it gently with her foot instead, having kicked the pillow outside the door to one side.

As she nudged the door open with her right hip, the wondrous notion that James might, in fact, be fast asleep passed over her. What a relief it would be to simply place the broth and compresses close by the bed and fly back out again like a good fairy in a fluttering of gossamer wings. James would never know she'd been there.

'Sal, is that you?' a voice croaked.

'Sugar lumps,' she murmured under her breath. Clearly there was to be no such luck today.

'I've brought you some soup and compresses,' she blurted out as she placed the bowl on his bedside table and the bucket at the foot of the bed, before taking a look at him properly.

Unlike Clare, who'd been flushed, James's face was ashen. Sally had never seen him look like this before and, for a moment, pure shock replaced all her anxieties. She wasn't sure which was worse.

'Thanks, Sal,' he murmured. 'I don't think I've ever felt this rotten.'

'Get well soon,' she replied, without meeting his eye. 'I best be off. More work than ever to be done today.'

'Stay a minute and chat to me,' James insisted, gesturing to the wooden chair in the corner of the small attic room. 'You're the first person I've seen since Mrs Hartley sent me back to bed. I've been going half-crazy cooped up in here on my own.'

Gingerly, Sally sat down and gave James the latest news on who had and hadn't succumbed to the fever so far and about Mrs Ackroyd's dismay at working with Bess now Ellie had taken ill.

'You've right cheered me up, Sal,' James said with a shaky chuckle. 'It feels like ages since we've had a good natter, you and me. You're a good lass, you know.' As he closed his eyes, Sally took the chance to scarper. She almost forgot to put the pillow back at the foot of his door.

Her chest was pounding as she made her way back down the stairs and a bizarre mixture of feelings were flooding through her veins.

She was relieved, of course, that the meeting was finally over and pleased that she, alone, had managed to lighten James's day. A persistent longing remained deep within her, however, and continued to lurk, no matter how hard she tried to overlook it.

She could never quite forget that her

love for James was as pointless as a candle in the rain. He'd never feel anything for her other than a brotherly tenderness as a fellow servant and friend. She was, as he said, 'a good lass' to him and would never be anything more.

The Fever Burns On

It took longer than everyone had hoped for order to return to Brackenfold Hall. The servants were sure that Dr Marshall's vapour oil had prevented the worst from happening to anyone, but there wasn't much anyone could do to stop the infection spreading round the staff.

As soon as Clare began to recover, Mrs Hartley herself took ill, followed swiftly by Mr Sykes. James, Ellie and several of the other household staff remained confined to their beds for a few more days.

Julian Fairclough eventually began to improve, but it was still impossible for the rest of the family to return as the Hall remained full of infection.

With the housekeeper and butler out of action and Nancy, Miss Amelia's lady maid, still away from home, Mrs Ackroyd stepped up temporarily as leader of the servants.

'Are the rugs clean, Sally?' she barked

one afternoon. 'Have you given Mrs Hartley her vapour oil?'

'Getting there, Mrs Ackroyd,' Sally had replied, rushing past her before the cook could give her any more orders. She still couldn't quite get used to seeing Mrs Ackroyd bustling around the corridors above stairs. In all the years she'd worked at the Hall, Sally wasn't sure she'd ever seen the cook anywhere in the house other than the kitchen and the servants' dining-room next door.

'She's a monster,' Bess muttered to Sally that night, as they got ready for bed. The scullery maid was normally the last to retire but, given the current circumstances, Sally had stayed up late to give her a hand scrubbing the pots clean for the next round of broth the following day.

Clare was almost back to normal now and had even started taking on a few light duties but Sally had yet to return to their bedroom in case she was still infectious.

Bess's tiny box-room had never

been intended for two inhabitants and the threadbare mattress they'd wedged against the wall was far from comfortable. Sally had to admit that she was looking forward to the day she could return to her good friend and familiar bed.

'I think she's quite enjoying the power,' Sally giggled, brushing out her locks of rich chestnut hair.

'She loves it,' Bess responded glumly. Her hair was thin, straight and mousy brown. She didn't bother brushing it before bed as it hardly ever tangled or became knotty. 'I thought Mrs Hartley was bad but I can't wait till she's fit and well again now.'

'Mrs Hartley is very fair,' Sally replied. 'The Hall's not a bad place to work, Bess. There's plenty of worse employers out there.'

Bess shrugged and gave a small sigh. Sally wondered whether this might be a good time to talk to Bess about her demeanour and gently suggest that adopting a sunnier disposition might result in better relations with the rest of the staff, but it was late and both girls were tired. She'd try to find a better time to talk to her when they both had a little more energy.

Bess always fell asleep quickly and it wasn't long before she began to snore softly. The noise wasn't loud enough to worry Sally, but still, she found that sleep was slow to come.

Why was it, she pondered, that Bess was finding it so difficult to settle in to life at the Hall? She'd arrived about a year ago at fourteen years old to take up the role of scullery maid but still felt very much the newcomer amongst the others.

'She's not a child any more,' Mrs Ackroyd had remarked recently when Bess was out of the room. 'You were her age too when you first came to the Hall, Sal, and we never saw any of that surly attitude from you.'

It was the closest the cook had ever come to giving Sally a compliment and in any other circumstance she would have been quite touched.

'I don't know, Mrs Ackroyd,' Sally had replied. 'I think it's just taking Bess a bit longer to feel confident here. She's of a very different nature to me.'

'She certainly is,' the cook replied, rolling her eyes.

Sally could still remember her first day at the Hall. Like Bess, she too had started at fourteen years old as the scullery maid and had been given the tiny box-room that Bess had now.

Sally had never spent a night away from home before. As a child of mill workers, hard graft was hardly a new concept but there was still no denying that the dawn starts and late night finishes had been something of a shock in the beginning.

Sally could distinctly remember weeping quietly for her little kitchen bed in her family's small mill cottage. Exhaustion and homesickness made for a cruel combination of feelings. It wasn't just the drudgery of the work, though — the role of the scullery maid was a solitary one.

As lowest in the servants' pecking

order, she was expected to be first to rise and the last to go to bed. She wasn't even allowed to eat at the staff table with everyone else but was to stay in the kitchen to make sure none of the food that was still cooking got burned.

As she continued to try and drift off into slumber, Sally thought on about how, in time, she'd overcome the loneliness and adjusted to the long hours at the Hall. True, she was naturally of a brighter disposition than Bess, and rather than rolling her eyes at the series of orders her superiors would shout down at her, she'd make the effort to go over and above their expectations.

There was something else, however, that had made the transition easier, Sally had to admit, and that was her friendship with James.

Clare hadn't yet joined the staff at Brackenfold when Sally had first started and whilst the others appreciated the respect she showed them and her attitude towards her work, they hadn't much in the way of friendship to offer her.

It was James who'd noticed her eyes welling up with tears, despite her eager smile, and the dark circles under her eyes from sheer lack of sleep.

'Cuppa for you, Sal,' he'd murmur when he'd pop in to see her after mealtimes whilst she was still stuck in the kitchen. He'd even help her scrub the kitchen surfaces, ovens and hobs sometimes when he wasn't too busy. It was important that everything was completely clean or mould and mildew would form which would put the food at risk of contamination.

Sally knew that he'd been kind to Bess, too, and generally made the effort to welcome all new recruits. He was thoughtful like that.

'Drat,' Sally muttered to herself as she wiped a stray tear from her eye. She hadn't meant to think of James and all that he meant to her as she tried to fall asleep.

Oblivion seemed further away than ever as she anguished over her unrequited love for the man who'd looked out for her as a new kid those five years ago.

No Running Away From It

'Our Sal!' Mary Halfpenny looked surprised and delighted as she flung open her front door to welcome her daughter to the cottage a few days later.

'You're not going to infect us, are you, Sal?' Fred called from inside the house, though he, too, looked happy to see his daughter.

'Well, Mrs Hartley said it was up to me if I wanted to take the risk, but everyone who took ill has almost recovered now and there haven't been any new cases for two or three days, so she said it'd probably be all right. Everyone's raving about the new vapour oil Dr Marshall gave everyone. It seems to have done the trick.'

It was a Saturday afternoon. Mrs Hartley, who was fully recovered herself, had told Sally that she might take a few hours off, given that she'd worked so hard during the past few weeks.

Life at the Hall was beginning to go

back to normal, though the family and the small contingent of servants they'd taken with them wouldn't return for at least a couple more days.

The weather remained very chilly and a thick layer of white mist was hanging over the Brackenfold valley.

The cold wind had felt raw as Sally had made her way over to her parents' cottage and the country roads held the murky smell of sodden mud.

She was glad to get inside and it felt so good to be back in the kitchen she'd grown up in, with its soapy smell of drying laundry and the crackle of the fire in the grate.

Fred Halfpenny sat on the one armchair they owned. It was a faded myrtle green and sunken in the middle with a couple of patches on it where the fabric had worn away. Mary had tried to find the same shade of green, but inevitably there was a bit of variation in colour. Sally had always loved that chair and took any opportunity to sit in when her father was out of the room.

Sally knew she'd been lucky to escape the fever but had to admit that the days making up the work for the rest of the servants had been hard. Her back and shoulders ached more than usual and she knew her eyes looked bloodshot and tired.

'You're not looking so well, Sal. I do hope you haven't caught anything,' her mother said as she set Sally's cup of tea in front of her and a slice of the Victoria sponge cake that Mary made so well. The cup was decorated with a dozen small song birds swooping through a pale blue sky. The sides were all chipped and the paint was fading but Sally loved it all the same.

'Thanks, Ma,' she replied. 'I'm worn out, that's all.'

'I've told you they work you too hard in that place, Sal,' came a voice. William, Sally's older brother, had appeared in the kitchen from upstairs. He went straight for the kettle on the range to pour himself a cup of tea too.

'You work for the Faircloughs as well,

Will,' Sally responded as she sipped her tea.

'Yes, but in the mill,' he answered quickly. 'I wouldn't wait on them for a living, that's for sure.'

'Oh, give over, Will!' Mary chimed in. 'I'd go back to the Hall tomorrow given half a chance!'

Sally knew that her mother had started at the Hall as a scullery maid aged only fourteen. Just like Sally, Mary had progressed to the role of housemaid after a couple of years.

It wasn't long after, however, that Mary had fallen for a young mill worker, Fred Halfpenny, whom she'd known since childhood, and they were married the following summer.

Mary joined her husband in the mill after their wedding. It wouldn't have done to live in separate lodgings to her new husband, of course, but Sally knew it had been hard for her mother to leave the Hall and the life she'd grown used to there. Mary had wanted roles in the Hall for her two children, but William was having none of it.

'There are opportunities in the mill, Ma,' he'd argued from a young age. 'I want to rise up the ranks and make something of myself.'

'It's dangerous, though, Will,' Sally had heard her mother protest. 'I've lost track of how many accidents I've seen on the looms. It's the youngest that do the most risky tasks, too. You'd be so much safer in the Hall.'

'I don't want to be safe, Ma,' William had replied. 'I want to be free to go to bed at whatever time I choose. I want to save my wages for a little cottage of my own one day. Who knows, I might even leave Brackenfold completely and travel further afield. I don't want to live in a draughty servant's bedroom for the rest of my life.'

'A servant's bedroom in the midst of a fine and wonderful house, the likes of which folk like us will never see in our lives,' Mary responded, though she knew it was a losing battle.

William point blank refused to work in

the Hall and as soon as he was allowed, he left the tiny schoolhouse in Brackenfold village and made straight for Fairclough's Mill.

'How are things at the Hall, Sal?' Mary asked, handing Sally an extra slice of cake for Clare for when she was feeling up to eating it. 'Aside from the fever, that is.'

'Oh, you know,' Sally replied. 'Mrs Ackroyd is exactly the same, as are all the other staff. Not much changes these days.'

'And James?' Mary asked, more gently this time.

'He's fully recovered, thank goodness,' Sally responded briskly as she avoided her mother's eye.

'He'll be looking forward to Nancy getting back, no doubt,' William chimed in. 'What was that look for, Ma?' he went on, looking puzzled. 'The whole village knows he's sweet on her.'

'If you'll excuse me, I need a breath of fresh air,' Sally announced, though truthfully, another cold blast of the February wind was the last thing on earth she fancied at that moment. Still, she needed to leave the room. She loved her family dearly but her mother's pity combined with the brutal honesty of her brother was more than she could cope with just now.

Sally had never told Mary of her feelings for James, but her mother had a natural skill in deciphering the truth, especially in matters of the heart.

Sally looked up at the sky. The mist had cleared, but dark and threatening rain clouds had gathered over the valley. It wasn't long before the first splashes of rain began to fall.

Sally took a deep breath and turned to the door to return to her family. It wouldn't do to catch a chill now, just as the worst of the fever had finally disappeared.

Once again, she tried hard to banish all thoughts of James from her mind and the agony of his feelings for Nancy, too. William had touched a nerve with his offhand remark. It bruised Sally's soul to face up to the reality of it, but there was simply no running away from it now.

For as long as anyone could remember, James had been thoroughly and unashamedly in love with Nancy Berry, Miss Amelia's lady's maid at Brackenfold Hall.

The Return of the Faircloughs

The day of the Faircloughs' return finally came round and, rather like the onslaught of the fever, a sense of panic whipped round the servants as they toiled long and hard to ensure the house was in a presentable state for the family's arrival home.

Mrs Hartley refused to settle for anything less than perfect, and expected sparkling cleanliness in every room of the Hall.

It was just as she was shaking out the ninth rug of the morning that Sally felt a tightening in her throat and a shiver pass down her neck. When she put her hand to her face, however, it felt unnaturally hot.

'Please no,' she murmured as she concentrated on the job in hand and tried to turn her mind to other things. It was no use, however, and by noon she'd taken to her bed.

'Just my luck,' she muttered as she

drifted in and out of a restless sleep. A thick fog was swirling round her brain and she struggled to think clearly. Sally's whole body felt drained of energy and consumed by vicious hot flames. She yearned for water but any sips she took reduced her to endless bouts of coughing. It wasn't long before her chest ached painfully from it.

'Some broth for you, Sal, and some of that oil Dr Marshall prescribed. Luckily there was a bit left over.' Sally opened her eyes and saw James standing at the door in his luncheon time livery suit.

'Where's Clare?' she croaked, sitting up as best she could in bed. It took an immense amount of effort and she descended into coughs again.

'I was chatting to Nancy now she's back and Mrs Hartley gave me a right rollicking for it,' James answered, his blue eyes misting over and his cheeks turning a little pink. He was fair-skinned with curls of sandy brown hair. Sally noticed how easily he coloured at even the mention of Nancy's name.

'She gave me a dozen more jobs to do and one of them was seeing to you,' James went on. 'That was the best chore of the lot,' he added with a wink. 'Now you best be back to your normal cheery self soon, lass. Mrs Hartley is convinced everyone will take ill again and we could all do without her worrying.'

Sally knew he wouldn't have taken the telling off personally. Mrs Hartley would never stay cross with him for long. She appreciated him far too much for that.

Sally managed a few tiny sips of soup after James had left her and it wasn't long before she'd collapsed into a dense and dreamless sleep as the infection rattled through her chest and seeped into every cell of her body.

★ ★ ★

'Morning, lovey.'

Sally opened her eyes to see Clare sitting by her bed with a fresh bowl of broth in her hands in a total role reversal. Sally's chest still felt tight and her body retained the fiery heat from yesterday but something was different. Her head felt clearer — much clearer in fact. The fog from yesterday had all but gone. It was such a relief to think properly again.

Sally felt ready to take some broth and even thought she might be able to manage a little bread, too.

'By heck, Sal, you're looking like yourself again.' Clare grinned. 'I could barely take a sip of broth when I was one day into the fever and you look ready to polish off the lot! Your face is brighter, too.'

'I don't feel half as bad as I thought I might,' Sally replied. 'Maybe I've got a different strain of the infection, a milder one, perhaps.'

'It certainly looks like it,' Clare said. 'Or it could be that an early dose of that vapour oil has sent the virus away. I don't think there'll be any need for me to move in with Bess after all, which is good as I didn't right fancy sharing with her.

'Still, I think you should stay in bed for at least the rest of the day. It's best to be on the safe side and Mrs Hartley won't want the infection spreading, even if it is a milder strain.'

'I suppose not,' Sally replied. 'What's it like today?'

'Mayhem,' Clare answered, rolling her eyes. 'I reckon the family are making up for lost time and are sending out invitations all over the place, so there's extra pressure to make sure everywhere is spotless.

'Nancy thinks that the Faircloughs are on the look-out for a suitable husband for Miss Amelia so are inviting the great and the good of Yorkshire over to make plans. No-one liked it in Rochdale, apparently, and they're very glad to be home. Rachel took ill whilst they were there and Nancy had to look after the little 'un as well as her usual duties.'

Rachel was nurse to Miss Florence, Julian and Grace's two-year-old daughter. Clare rolled her eyes again.

'You'd think it was slave labour by the way she moaned on about it. I don't think Nancy's got much patience with young children. Miss Amelia's given her yet another cast-off dress to say thank you for the extra work. It's an emerald green one this time. She was flouncing about in it last night at teatime.'

'I bet James couldn't take his eyes off her,' Sally said quietly. Clare gave a sympathetic shrug and quickly changed the subject.

'Mrs Ackroyd has been sent over a dozen dinner orders for the coming fortnight and I think she's feeling the pressure. Her mood has gone from bad to worse.'

'Goodness,' Sally answered. She knew her absence would be adding considerably to Clare's workload. 'I'll make sure I'm fit again soon.'

'Don't be daft, Sal,' Clare said, pretending to look stern. 'You did the same for me when I was poorly. Now, I best be off. I wouldn't be surprised if Mrs Hartley is timing me!'

Sally lay back in bed once Clare had gone. She could see pearly white clouds floating through a pale blue sky through the small window pane of the attic bedroom and the occasional bird swoop by.

The weather seemed to have turned a corner and Sally hoped spring might finally be on its way.

She tried to relax and make the most of the unexpected break from work but somehow her thoughts kept floating back to Nancy in Miss Amelia's unwanted dress as she basked in the admiration of every young man in the servants' quarters. She'd have soaked up their attention like a late blooming daffodil flourishing in the springtime sun.

It wasn't often that Sally saw Miss Amelia or any of the Fairclough family around the Hall. With their own staff staircase and an entrance just for them, the servants mostly kept out of the way, neither seen nor heard by the family.

Their strict timetable of duties ensured the rooms were cleaned when they weren't in use by the Faircloughs so it was a rare happening for the two worlds to collide.

Exceptions were village celebrations like May Day and the Rushbearing festival in late summer. Such occasions were an opportunity for everyone to get together, regardless of their station in life.

From days like these and the occasional glimpse she'd catch of Miss Amelia, Sally knew the mistress was striking in her beauty and coquettish in her charm. She'd often flick her curls which bounced as she walked and her smile was full of mischievous fun.

From Nancy's tales of suitors falling at Miss Amelia's feet, Sally was fairly sure the lady's maid emulated her mistress's behaviour and sought to be like her in all things.

It wasn't unusual for Miss Amelia to pass on last season's clothes to her maid. She was known to be quite generous in that regard. Nancy would be given the odd sash too, and, once, an elegant gold brooch made with three misty white opal stones surrounding a single pearl, resembling a clover.

Nancy took great pride in telling the rest of the staff that the clover was a symbol of femininity and virtue. The other girls eyed the piece enviously whilst Mrs Ackroyd tutted under her breath.

Sarah, lady's maid to the older Mrs Fairclough, would share any treasures her mistress gave her with the rest of the girls in the Hall. It never occurred to Nancy to do any such thing, however. She delighted in keeping her bounty all to herself.

'She thinks she's born to higher things, that one,' Mrs Ackroyd would often mutter when Nancy was out of earshot.

'Don't be jealous,' James would reply. He wasn't inclined to argue and was generally good-natured in debates, but Sally knew he'd always stand up for Nancy and would only ever see the best in her.

One of the hardest things was that Sally could understand his admiration. Nancy's lustrous long mane of hair reminded her of rich, warm honey and her dimpled cheeks were dusted with a light sprinkling of freckles. Her green eyes danced when she laughed and she was quick to see humour in even the toughest of days at the Hall.

'She's our ray of sunshine,' Mr Sykes had said once. He didn't hand out compliments quickly and was generally of a very serious disposition but Nancy brought out the softer side of him.

There was something about the lady's maid, however, that troubled Sally. She was sure it was more than mere envy, too. If she set her feelings for James to one side, Sally still couldn't find any liking for the girl.

Perhaps it was the fact that Nancy never said thank you when James brought her cup of tea to her in the servants' dining-room or possibly it was the time he brought her a freshly cut bunch of flowers from the grounds and she left them wilting on the window-sill without even putting them in water.

Nancy Berry was one careless soul, Sally decided, as she drifted off into a midmorning nap. Even if she was destined never to win his heart, Sally still thought James deserved a sweetheart who could return his affections with a vigour equal to his own.

Tension in the Air

Feeling almost her usual self once more and fortified by the extra rest, Sally returned to her duties the following day. As usual, she and Clare rose soon after dawn to start cleaning out the grates, ready for the day ahead.

Next, Sally moved on to the drawing-room, where there was lots of dusting to be done and, despite her quick recovery, she soon found herself in a constant bout of sneezes as the dust circulated in the air.

Even so, she made sure every ornament and artefact looked as perfect as the day they were made. Sally had always taken great pride in her work, no matter how uncomfortable it could be.

Still, it was a relief when the dusting was finished and it was time to head into the dining-room to make a start on polishing the silverware. The grand solid oak dining table had half a dozen large candlesticks on it which all needed a good clean, plus there was the cutlery to see to as well. She'd be busy right up to midday.

It wasn't long before her arms and wrists were aching from the intensity of the work, but it was satisfying to see the candlesticks gleaming as they caught the morning sunbeams shining in from the large bay windows which overlooked the Hall's extensive grounds.

The flower-beds were carpeted in crocuses which formed a pastel patchwork of colour all over the gardens. Sally was so glad the spring flowers had finally arrived and hummed very quietly to herself as she carried on with her work.

Every so often she'd raise her head to look up at the intricately painted ceiling. Anyone would have thought that after five years at the Hall, she'd have grown used to the delicate mauve of the floral patterns, the leafy greens of the trees and the golden gowns of the fair maidens as they lounged in the idyllic countryside. Some were playing musical instruments whilst others worked on embroidery.

Sally knew she could lose herself for hours in that make-believe world overhead, but would only allow herself the briefest of glances. Daydreaming wasn't a luxury on offer to the servants of Brackenfold Hall.

At one point, she heard some fast steps pattering along the corridor and what sounded like a frantic exchange of voices, but they'd gone before she could investigate further and, anyway, it was far too nice a morning to worry about whatever might have come to pass. She'd find out soon, no doubt, and Mrs Hartley was sure to have everything under control in a jiffy.

Sally was just finishing off the last of the cutlery when the tall and stocky figure of James appeared, ready to set the table for the family's luncheon. He filled the dining-room doorway.

'All right, Sal,' he said quietly.

'Goodness, is it lunch time already?' Sally answered. 'I'm all finished now and will get out of your hair.'

'No rush,' he replied. His tone was low

and there was none of his usual joviality to be seen today. James's brow was all furrowed too and there was worry in his glassy blue eyes.

'Is something wrong?' Sally asked. Her voice was quiet too.

'It's Nance,' he answered. 'She's in a right state. You remember that brooch the mistress gave her, don't you, Sal? The one in the shape of a flower?'

'A clover. Yes, I do,' Sally replied.

'Well, she can't find it anywhere,' James said. 'She's looked high and low but no joy whatsoever.'

'She doesn't think . . . ' Sally stopped, thinking back to those fast-paced steps and frantic voices from earlier on.

James ran a hand through his hair and for a while neither of them said anything.

'It's beginning to look like it's been pinched,' he said eventually. 'Nancy's convinced we have a thief among us.'

★ ★ ★

The atmosphere amongst the servants was strained for the rest of the day. Nancy didn't come downstairs for anything to eat during the servants' lunch break. James said she was too upset. He ate his food quickly and barely spoke to anyone else before disappearing upstairs with a cup of sweet tea and a slice of buttered toast for her.

'Where on earth could that brooch be?' Ellie asked once James had gone.

'She'll find it soon enough,' Mrs Hartley replied. 'I expect it's under a pile of clothes somewhere in her bedroom. She mentioned the other day that she hasn't had time to unpack properly since she arrived home from Rochdale.'

'Let's hope so,' Ellie answered, though her eyes were fixed on the doorway to the kitchen where Bess had appeared with her arms crossed and her shoulders slouched.

'The soup's boiling now, Mrs Ackroyd,' she said quietly. 'Shall I take it off the hob?'

'I don't know why you can't use your

initiative, child,' the cook said irritably. 'I shouldn't have to repeat the same instructions to you over and over again.'

'Well, you said I'd got it wrong last time,' Bess replied. 'So I thought I'd best check.'

'So insolent,' Mrs Ackroyd muttered as she finished the last of her pie. The scullery maid had disappeared off back into the kitchen.

'Sorry, Mrs Ackroyd, I know I'm late,' came a breathless voice. Rachel, the nurse, had just rushed into the kitchen. She was a pretty young woman with a rounded figure, wavy blonde hair and rosy cheeks. Rachel was usually very neatly turned out but today her hair was falling out of her cap and what looked like a little piece of broccoli was nestling in her curls.

Mrs Ackroyd tutted and rolled her eyes, but still waved Rachel into the kitchen to collect some of the remaining pie.

'I didn't think Miss Florence was ever going to finish eating,' Rachel said, once she'd caught her breath, straightened herself up and taken a sip of water. 'I think she threw most of it at me.'

The other servants didn't see much of the nursemaid as she was always so busy with her charge, though as the Faircloughs usually liked to spend a small amount of time with the two-year-old after Rachel had given her some luncheon and tidied her up. The nursemaid was generally allowed 20 minutes or so to eat her own meal with the rest of the servants downstairs.

'Is she still refusing to eat vegetables?' Sally asked.

'Absolutely,' Rachel replied. 'She's taken against anything green, which is unfortunate when the garden is full of broccoli and savoy cabbage at the moment. Her mother is adamant that Miss Florence needs the nourishment of the spring vegetables, which is all well and good, but she's not the one who has to coax them into her mouth.'

The servants all offered their sympathies whilst Mrs Hartley spoke of Mr

Julian's refusal to eat anything other than potatoes when he was a similar age. She had been at the Hall longer than any of them.

Sally was glad of the change in topic and found herself offering possible strategies to help Rachel with her wilful young charge. It was pleasant to forget the missing brooch, even if it was only for a few minutes.

The tension, however, had returned by teatime that evening. Nancy did manage to make it downstairs this time but her face was swollen and her eyes were bloodshot from crying. She still managed to look beautiful though, even in this much despair.

'I'm really sorry to hear about your brooch, Nancy,' Sally had said as the lady's maid appeared in the kitchen doorway. Nancy barely acknowledged the remark as she made her way over to her seat beside James.

'Thanks, Sal,' he murmured on her behalf.

'Try and manage a bit more, dear,'

Mrs Hartley said half an hour or so later as Nancy pushed her stew round her plate.

'I'm not hungry,' she whispered. 'I feel like I might be sick.'

'She's right, Nance,' James said, placing his hand on her shoulder for a moment. 'I know it's hard, but you've got to eat.'

'That brooch was the finest thing I ever owned,' Nancy blurted out angrily. 'I'd never seen anything so beautiful.'

'The likes of us don't have fancy jewels, lass,' Mrs Ackroyd said in a low voice. 'Pretend you never had it in the first place. It's the easiest way.' James shot the cook a look of exasperation as fresh tears welled in Nancy's eyes.

Just then there was a loud crash from the kitchen.

'Goodness,' Mrs Ackroyd cried, rising from her chair. 'What on earth's going on in there, Bess?'

'Just dropped a pan,' Bess called back. 'No need to yell at me this time.'

'Now I think about it, she's the only one who hasn't told me she's sorry about my brooch,' Nancy said suddenly, as Mrs Ackroyd sat back down at the table. The lady's maid had sat up in her chair now and was looking alert for the first time that evening. There was a long and uncomfortable pause. Sally found herself unable to look up from her plate.

'Well now, Bess doesn't say a great deal to any of us,' Mrs Hartley remarked eventually.

'No, she keeps herself to herself all right,' Mrs Ackroyd said. Her tone was low and full of suspicion. 'Nothing went missing before she arrived.' Sally stared down at her half eaten stew. Like Nancy, she had completely lost her appetite.

After a minute or so, she managed to look up at the others. James had his head in his hands whilst everyone else looked confused and unhappy as well.

'That's quite enough,' Mrs Hartley said firmly. 'There will be no accusations in this house without any evidence.'

At that moment, Sally thought she heard a muffled sob from the kitchen and the pattering of feet.

'The walls down here are thin, remember,' Mrs Hartley added sternly before standing up to leave the table. Clearly she had heard the cry too.

A Word of Warning

'Wasn't teatime awful?' Sally commented to Clare as they got ready for bed that evening. They were both brushing out their hair.

'I know,' Clare replied. 'I didn't know where to look. Your curls are all knotty again, Sal. Would you like me to try and get them out?'

'Yes, please.' Sally was always grateful for Clare's help with her hair which usually got tangled after a day tied up under her maid's cap. She loved her long, thick curly locks but they weren't very practical when it came to day-to-day life.

'What do you think happened to the brooch?' Clare asked as she got started on one of the knots. Clare's own hair was dark, straight and glossy. It never knotted up or became tangled.

'I honestly don't know,' Sally answered, wincing slightly as the brush attacked a particularly stubborn tangle. 'But Nancy can't go around accusing Bess. That's so unfair.'

'I agree with you, Sal,' Clare said slowly. 'I just wish she'd try a bit harder with us and that way they wouldn't be so quick to suspect her.'

'Poor lass,' Sally murmured. She was feeling tired now and Clare had almost finished smoothing all the knots out.

It wasn't long before both girls were tucked up in their beds with the candle blown out. Before she drifted off, it struck Sally how lucky she was to have Clare.

She may have been unlucky in love but she knew the bond she shared with her best friend was something very special and rare. It made the long hours and drudgery bearable, too. Sally hoped with all her heart that Bess might find a chum of her own one day. It wouldn't do anyone any good to be as solitary as she was.

★ ★ ★

Nancy remained weepy and subdued for the rest of the week and the atmosphere amongst the servants stayed strained too.

Sally spotted James scouring the corridor floors and checking behind curtains whenever he could find the time and she knew he was still hoping the brooch would turn up so the whole thing could be forgotten.

Bess was quieter than ever and kept out of everybody's way. Sally had to make an extra effort to seek her out but usually managed to catch her after the servants' evening meal and made sure she sat with her for five minutes or so whilst Bess tended to the steaming pots on the hob.

'It was nice and bright today,' Sally commented one evening. It was hard to get much of a conversation out of Bess and she often resorted to making general remarks about the weather.

'S'pose,' Bess replied gloomily. 'Don't get to see much of it down here.'

'When's your next day off?'

'Sat'day,' Bess answered as she peered

at a joint of beef which was roasting in one of the ovens. 'In the morning.'

'Doing owt nice?'

'I'll just head over to Ma's to see how she and our Meg are doing.'

'That's good,' Sally said with a smile. She'd often seen Bess trudging over to her mother's cottage in the village when she had any time off. 'How is your ma now?'

Sally knew that Mrs Trimble hadn't been in good health for some time. She suffered with aches all over her body and rarely went outdoors.

'Not well,' Bess responded. 'She's hardly getting out of bed these days.'

'Oh, I'm so sorry, Bess,' Sally said. The scullery maid shrugged and avoided Sally's eye.

'It's our Meg I feel sorry for,' she said eventually. 'She's all Ma's got now I'm here. The bit of money I make helps but she's the one who has to care for Ma. They're both cooped up inside all the time. Ma doesn't like being on her own. She's bad with her nerves now, see?'

'How hard for your sister,' Sally said quietly. To her dismay, Bess was angrily rubbing tears from her eyes.

'I'm just so worried,' she gasped out eventually, 'about both of them.'

'You're doing all you can, lovey,' Sally whispered and placed a hand over Bess's red and chapped one before leaving the kitchen. She couldn't help but glare at Nancy and Ellie who were whispering on the other side of the kitchen.

'If only they knew,' she muttered furiously to herself as she went upstairs to restart her work.

*　*　*

Mrs Hartley's face was stern the following morning at breakfast. Sally had only just finished her porridge and tea when the housekeeper announced that she would like a word with every member of staff at the Hall.

'Right,' she began, once everyone was listening. 'I've said it before and I'll say it again. I would like to make it absolutely clear that there are to be no unfounded allegations in this house towards any member of my staff.'

Sally looked about her. Nancy was staring at the floor whilst James stood close beside her. Bess was standing at the kitchen door blank-faced. Mrs Ackroyd was standing next to Mrs Hartley and Mr Sykes in what appeared to be a united front from the senior members of staff, which Sally found rather ironic.

'Any concerns are to come directly to me,' Mrs Hartley went on. 'And without some tangible evidence I will not be taking heed of anything you have to tell me. Personal dislikes, unsubstantiated suspicions and circumstantial events have no place here. Is that understood?'

'Yes, Mrs Hartley,' the staff murmured in reply.

'Pardon?'

'Yes, Mrs Hartley,' came a louder response. Sally heard her voice ring out louder than anybody else's.

'We have a gentleman visitor arriving at the Hall next week,' Mrs Hartley added. 'His name is Mr Wainscot, a wealthy industrialist and land owner from somewhere down south. We think he's a possible suitor for Miss Amelia. He will be bringing his valet with him who will be our guest downstairs. Let's try to show him that we're a decent set of people, shall we?' Mrs Hartley's voice remained low and stern. 'Now, be off with you all. There's plenty of work to be done.'

Sally caught the housekeeper's eye as she made her way to the servants' steps on her way upstairs.

She had been sure she'd done the right thing by going to Mrs Hartley the previous evening with her worries for Bess. It wouldn't have been perceptible to anyone else but Sally was sure that when their eyes met, Mrs Hartley's head tilted in the smallest of nods.

The Guest

Sally could hear loud voices and chatting right from the top of the stairs as she made her way down the servants' steps for lunch a few days later. It was never normally this noisy downstairs.

It had been a long morning and Sally's nose was full of dust from all the rugs she'd shaken out. Her breakfast felt like a very long time ago and she was starving. The weather was miserable, too. It had rained steadily since dawn.

'Sally,' Mrs Hartley greeted her at the foot of the stairs. She looked rather different today, Sally noticed. There was a brightness in her eyes and cheeks that Sally hadn't seen for some time. 'Come and meet our guest, Mr Wainscot's valet. He's very charming.'

Sally turned into the staff dining-room to find Ellie, Rachel, Clare, Nancy and several other members of staff laughing merrily at something the raven-haired stranger was saying. He was lounging languidly at the head of the table, where the cook usually sat for meals.

Sally risked a look at Mrs Ackroyd, who was sitting in the next seat along. It was remarkably brave for anyone to usurp her usual perch. None of the regular staff would have dared.

The cook, however, didn't look upset at all. In fact, she was hanging on the stranger's every word. Her eyes were sparkling and at one point she even gave a high-pitched girlish giggle at something he said. Sally wasn't sure she'd ever heard Mrs Ackroyd laugh like that before. The cook barely cracked a smile most days.

'This is Sally, our housemaid,' Mrs Hartley said as Sally took her place at the table and helped herself from the large pot of soup in the centre of the table. 'And this is Mr Richard Crookshanks.'

'Very nice to meet you, Sally,' Mr Crookshanks answered, nodding in her direction. 'Everyone at Brackenfold has been so friendly so far and this soup is delicious, Mrs Ackroyd.'

'Oh, it's very easy to rustle up,' the

cook replied, glowing with pride. She was completely oblivious to the indignant tut of derision from Ellie who'd been slaving over it all morning.

As she buttered a slice of bread, Sally took a moment to properly take in their new guest. She'd read about 'tall, dark and handsome' men, in the cheap romantic novels and magazines she shared with Clare, but had never actually seen such a person in real life.

Even seated, Mr Crookshanks was clearly a head taller than most of the other staff. His dark hair was attractively styled in a slight wave. He was clean-shaven, too, which highlighted his high cheekbones and his pale but healthy-looking skin. His deep-set eyes were a startling shade of blue.

He looked more like a gentleman than a valet. It was as if a member of the gentry had appeared below stairs and Sally felt curiously uprooted and confused.

A subtle nudge from Clare beside her told Sally that she was gawping, so she tried as far as she could to concentrate on her soup and bread.

'My master and I love travelling,' Mr Crookshanks was saying. His voice sounded more refined than their Yorkshire accents, too. He was from somewhere in the south of England called Salisbury. Even the serving classes clearly spoke very well down there. 'We've been to Scotland, France and even America.'

'You never have!' Ellie squealed. 'What was America like?'

'Sensational.' Mr Crookshanks grinned in reply. His eyes were sparkling more than ever as he spoke of the bustling and prosperous island of Manhattan with its vast array of theatres, opera houses, shops and stylish people literally dripping with wealth.

'I'd love to go somewhere like that,' Nancy said from across the table. She was beginning to look like herself again, despite the fact that there was still no news of her missing brooch.

'I've never been further than Leeds,' Ellie added, her soup and bread forgotten.

'Everyone should travel,' Mr Crookshanks said as he helped himself to more bread.

'Oh yes, I couldn't agree more. I've heard it stretches the mind,' Mrs Ackroyd replied, beaming. Sally turned her head away from the cook in an attempt to suppress her mirth. Thankfully, at that moment, her nose finally decided it had had enough of the dust from the morning, and gave way to a fit of sneezes, which nicely disguised her amusement.

One look at James's face after she'd recovered told her that he was thinking exactly the same thing. The cook was known for her deep-seated mistrust in anything and anyone that didn't originate from Yorkshire. She didn't even like Lancashire cheese. Sally was almost certain she'd never left the county.

'There's the most wonderful park in New York,' Mr Crookshanks went on. 'It's a haven of greenery in the centre of one of the busiest cities in the world. There are monuments, fountains and lakes packed full of lilies. It's just magi-cal.'

It might have been the spring rain lash-ing against the windows, or maybe the angry clouds shrouding the valley sides or perhaps it was simply their tired limbs aching from the daily grind, but in that moment Sally felt sure that every serv-ant in the dining-room was imagining themselves thousands of miles away in an exciting new world where dawn starts and Yorkshire weather were nowhere to be found.

★ ★ ★

'That Crookshanks fellow's a right show off,' James muttered to Sally when she passed him in the corridor later that afternoon.

'He's very talkative,' Sally answered tactfully, clutching her bottle of polish and duster.

'He loves the sound of his own voice, all right,' James replied with a grimace. 'I'm sure I heard Mr Sykes say that he'd read in a newspaper that the grand park in New York is only an idea at the moment. I think the valet has read about it and is making it all up as he goes along.

'I don't trust him,' he added as he hurried away.

The servants could never chat for long, especially on a busy day like this. The Faircloughs were entertaining Mr Wainscot so required an extra level of service from their staff. Sally was on her way to the library to make sure there was no dust lurking on any of the shelves, particularly the ones at the top, which were often neglected.

On entering the high-ceilinged room, Sally felt a comforting sense of tranquillity wash over her, as it always did when she came to the library.

It was a large room, but with its numerous bookshelves, velvety-brown easy chairs and delicately patterned Persian rugs over the shiny oak floors, it had a cosiness that Sally had always adored and a comforting smell of parchment mingled with cigar smoke.

The books were all too complicated for Sally to read, even if she'd been allowed to borrow one, but still, she liked to look at the titles as she worked.

'What D'ye Think Of The World?' and ''Twas Wrong To Marry Him,' were two of her favourites. As she methodically wiped each shelf, blowing the dust off the spines of the books as she did so, Sally let her thoughts turn to their visitor and the strange effect he'd had on the rest of the staff.

She'd never seen Mrs Ackroyd respond so positively to a newcomer before. She generally regarded them as an unwelcome liability. The rest of the staff seemed charmed too, with the exception of James, that is.

I wonder if he's scared Nancy's head has been turned, Sally thought as she climbed the ladder up to the higher shelves.

The dust was worse up here than she'd expected and it wasn't long before she started sneezing again. Thankfully she had remembered her pocket handkerchief.

Mr Crookshanks had striking good looks, after all, and his tales were quite out of the ordinary.

James shouldn't worry, though, Sally thought, as a big gust of dust blew into her eyes and blinded her for a second. Mr Crookshanks would be gone in a few days' time.

She wiped her eyes as the dust was making them water.

And anyway, it takes more than a few stories and a handsome face to change a heart, she decided. That valet, handsome though he is, is nothing compared to James.

The dust had all but gone now, but Sally found that her eyes were still weeping at the thought of her unrequited love.

Too Good to be True

Breakfast the following day brought more tales of high adventure from Mr Crookshanks. This time he spoke of the time he and Mr Wainscot rode camels in Egypt and saw the famous pyramids.

'They're one of the Seven Wonders of the World, you know,' he said as he sprinkled brown sugar over his porridge.

'Wasn't it too hot?' a voice asked.

Sally, along with the rest of the servants looked up to see Bess standing at the kitchen door. There was a moment of silence. Bess rarely spoke unless directly addressed and for her to ask a question like this, in front of everyone else, had never been known before.

'Oh, Bess, be off with you back to the pans,' Mrs Ackroyd said impatiently as the scullery maid coloured and then hurried away. 'Don't mind her,' she went on, turning to Mr Crookshanks. Her tone turned from irritated to doting in an instant. 'She's ever so insolent.'

Their guest, however, looked surprised.

'I've no objection to anyone asking questions,' he said. 'Miss!' he called out into the kitchen.

'Her name's Bess,' Sally said quietly beside him.

'Miss Bess!' he called out again. There was another pause. The whole table had gone silent. Mrs Ackroyd looked stunned and two spots of russet red, far deeper than the usual ruddiness of her complexion, had appeared on each of her cheeks.

After a short while, the scullery maid's slight figure appeared once again at the kitchen door. Her cheeks were still flushed.

'The sunshine was baking,' Mr Crookshanks said to her with an easy smile, completely oblivious to the tension around him. 'My skin burned under its hot rays but still, I'd take that over a wet and blustery day in Yorkshire, wouldn't you?'

'Yes,' Bess whispered. Sally saw the beginnings of a smile flickering on her thin lips before she darted back into the kitchen.

'Me, too,' Nancy announced, breaking the silence round the table. 'To be honest, though, I'd prefer to be anywhere than Brackenfold right now.'

★ ★ ★

The day wore on and the chores were as relentless as ever. Sally's morning consisted of mopping every corridor floor in the Hall. She returned to the servants' dining-room at midday feeling utterly exhausted. Every limb in her body was aching and she had a headache.

It was something of a relief that Mr Crookshanks was nowhere to be seen. Sally wondered if he was busy with a task set by Mr Wainscot. As interesting as his stories were, Sally's head was throbbing and she was grateful for a bit of quiet. She was just recovering over a cup of tea with some bread and dripping when Mrs Ackroyd called out to Bess in the kitchen.

'How's the sponge cake looking, Bess?'

'It's, um, all right, Mrs Ackroyd,' Bess replied, appearing at the door. She looked a bit flustered but there was a shine in her eyes that Sally hadn't seen before and the beginnings of the smile she'd seen earlier that day hadn't disappeared just yet either.

'Well, is it rising?' the cook asked impatiently. Sally wondered if she was still feeling piqued by their guest's display of support for the scullery maid and was taking it out on Bess. Mrs Ackroyd didn't take kindly to being shown up.

'Not yet,' Bess replied. Sally was sure she could hear a giggle bubbling in the scullery maid's throat. Mrs Ackroyd rolled her eyes and shook her head.

'Will you do me a favour, Sal, and pop in to see how she's doing after you've finished eating? Ellie's busy with the pastries and your ma makes a good sponge, doesn't she?'

'Yes, Mrs Ackroyd,' Sally replied. She'd always loved helping her mother with baking when she still lived with her family and liked to think that she'd picked up some of Mary's skills. It would be a welcome change from mopping, that was for sure.

Sally couldn't quite believe it when she stepped into the kitchen a few minutes later. For there, in one of Mrs Ackroyd's white aprons over his smart suit, poring over a big mixing bowl and recipe book with Bess, was Mr Crookshanks.

Ellie, who was rolling out pastry on the other side of the room, had a very strange expression on her face. Sally couldn't tell if it was suspicion, jealousy or disbelief, but the kitchen maid couldn't take her eyes off them.

'Is everything all right, Bess?' Sally asked.

'Oh yes,' she replied, glowing with happiness. That flicker of a smile had turned into a shining beam now. 'Well, it is now that Mr Crookshanks is helping me.'

'I'm quite enjoying it,' the valet said breezily. 'Mr Wainscot's out taking the air with the Faircloughs now it's finally stopped raining, so I've got a bit of spare time.

'Everyone laughed at my mother when

she taught me how to bake, but she must have known I'd find a use for it one day.'

'I don't know what I would have done if you hadn't been here to help me,' Bess said, still smiling. Her cheeks were dusted with a bit of flour from the mixture which made her seem even younger than normal.

'Don't mention it.' Mr Crookshanks laughed. 'It was an easy mistake to make. The two packets look just the same. They really should write a warning or something on the front.'

Sally shot Ellie a questioning look. The kitchen maid beckoned her over.

'Bess put carbolic soap in the cake mix,' Ellie whispered. 'I realised just as she was pouring it in.' Ellie paused and looked a little sheepish. 'Mrs Ackroyd asked me to put the soap straight in the dresser drawer as soon as we unpacked the groceries. The packet does look very similar to baking powder, see? I was busy and forgot, so it's my fault, too, I suppose.'

Ellie didn't say, but Sally felt sure her

role in this mistake had stopped her from going straight to the cook to tell on Bess.

'She burst into tears as soon as she realised,' Ellie went on, 'as naturally the mixture had to go in the bin. It was then that Mr Crookshanks just happened to be passing by and swooped in to save her by helping her make a new mix double-quick. There seems to be no end to his talents.'

There was something about Ellie's tone which told Sally the kitchen maid was starting to doubt their visitor. Her admiration for him had quickly dissolved.

Sally looked back at Bess as she poured the new mix into a baking tin ready for the oven. Thankfully she hadn't heard anything Ellie had said and there was nothing but wonder in her eyes.

Stuff and Nonsense

The servants' quarters were noticeably quieter after the departure of Mr Wainscot and his valet a few days later.

'So long, friends,' Mr Crookshanks had called to them all after breakfast as he left to load Mr Wainscot's belongings on to the carriage for their journey back to Salisbury.

Sally noticed Bess waving to him from the kitchen door and thought she saw a flash of something yellow in the scullery maid's hands but when she looked again, Bess had disappeared back into the kitchen.

'Do you think Mr Wainscot will be back to see Miss Amelia any time soon?' Mrs Ackroyd asked Nancy hopefully. She had clearly forgiven the valet for taking Bess's side, though Sally was sure she didn't know about the near miss with the cake.

Mr Crookshanks had re-joined his master and the mixture was safely in the oven by the time the cook returned to the kitchen. Sally certainly hadn't told the cook anything and she had a feeling that Ellie hadn't, either.

'I wouldn't have thought so,' Nancy replied flatly. 'To be honest, it seems Mr Wainscot was the direct opposite of his valet and wasn't very engaging at all. Plus he's balding, a little portly and wears a cologne so strong it's really quite overpowering. Miss Amelia told me that he was the most dreadful bore and she was glad to have seen the back of him.'

The servants all laughed apart from Mrs Ackroyd who huffed in disappointment and marched back in the kitchen to bark some orders at Ellie and Bess. James looked visibly relieved.

'I've been meaning to ask,' Nancy went on, 'has anyone seen a yellow ribbon? I went to tie up my hair this morning but found it had gone from my dressing table.'

The servants all turned to each other with blank faces, shrugs and shakes of the head.

'I'll keep a look out for it,' James said eventually. 'We all will.'

'Thanks,' Nancy answered. 'I'm having no luck at the moment. It may just be a ribbon, but it's very dear to me as my ma gave it to me last year. I seem to lose all my treasures right now.'

James murmured something sympathetic and reassured her again that everyone would help look.

'Miss Amelia will have to find a husband sometime,' Mrs Hartley said, changing the subject, as she sat back down at the kitchen table to finish her cup of tea. 'The young lady's nearly twenty years old.'

'She doesn't like anyone her family finds,' Nancy replied as she made her way to the steps to go upstairs. 'Personally I think she wants to go to London next year for the social season.

'I can't say I blame her. There are fine houses, dances, the opera, the most up to date fashions and folk from the nobility there too. Just think!' Nancy looked significantly happier at the idea.

'Miss Amelia will have a shock if she thinks the likes of the nobility will be interested in her,' Mrs Hartley said once Nancy had departed. 'She's the daughter of a wealthy clothier, not a lord. She may be revered up here but that won't be the case if she goes to London. There are the highest of the high everywhere round there. Miss Amelia has no idea.'

* * *

'Do you miss Mr Crookshanks?' Sally asked Clare as they got ready for bed that evening. Clare was smoothing out the knots in Sally's hair once again.

'Not really, Sal,' Clare replied. 'I mean, he was very handsome and all that, and his stories were entertaining, but I can't help but think he was a little bit in love with himself, if you know what I mean!'

'I think we all came to that realisation.' Sally giggled. 'Apart from Mrs Ackroyd and Bess, of course.' Clare giggled, too. Sally had already told her the story of the cake.

'I can't say I've ever been in love, Sal,' Clare said quietly. 'But if I do ever find a man for me, I think I'd want him to be, well, ordinary, like us, if you know what I mean. I'd be more impressed with a good cup of tea than tall tales from the high seas. Does that make me boring?'

'Well if it does, that makes two of us,' Sally replied, thinking once more of her feelings for James. 'I'm exactly the same as you.'

★ ★ ★

''S'cuse me, Sal,' came a voice the next morning. Sally had had a tiring start to the day laying fires and was glad of her porridge and tea. She looked up to see Bess standing next to her.

'What are you doing in here, Bess?' Mrs Ackroyd asked crossly before Sally had a chance to answer.

'Everything's in order, Mrs Ackroyd,' Bess answered promptly with a smile. 'I'll be back in the kitchen in a jiffy.'

'Good job,' the cook said, looking

rather surprised. It wasn't unusual for the scullery maid to answer her back, but she'd done so a lot more politely this time.

Sally had thought that the scullery maid might revert to her previous demeanour now Mr Crookshanks had left, but it would appear that something had changed. She had a new-found confidence that no-one had ever seen before. Sally was glad to see that her smile hadn't disappeared, either.

'Sal,' Bess said again. This time they weren't interrupted. 'I was wondering if you might help me with my letters. You're good at reading and writing, aren't you?'

'Not really, but I get by,' Sally answered, feeling quite flattered. She had enjoyed going to the Brackenfold schoolhouse when she was younger and would have gladly have stayed longer but, as her brother William never tired of pointing out, a good education didn't pay the bills, which Sally knew only too well.

'Of course I will,' she said in answer to Bess. Mrs Ackroyd raised an eyebrow.

'We'll try and find time when we're both off duty,' Sally added.

'You two have no need for books and writing,' the cook cut in. 'All that isn't for the likes of us, you know.'

'Perhaps not, Mrs Ackroyd, but that doesn't mean it's not worth having a go,' Sally answered. 'We have the right to better ourselves same as everybody else.' Bess nodded enthusiastically whist the cook simply shook her head.

'Stuff and nonsense,' she muttered to herself.

★ ★ ★

'You're doing really well,' Sally commented to Bess a few days later. She'd taken to joining Bess in her room after work had finished for the day to read a little of a magazine or novel by candle-light. Both girls were tired, of course, so they rarely managed longer than ten minutes.

Sally was pleased to see that Bess was able to read quite well and they both

enjoyed, in particular, the serialised stories that appeared each week in magazines
like 'Household Words'.

Usually, she would read aloud first
whilst Bess followed the words with
her finger and then they swapped. Sally
would then help Bess with anything that
proved difficult.

'Thanks, Sal, I'm right enjoying it.'
She grinned. 'I've never thought I had
time for stories but a good one really
brightens your day, doesn't it?'

'It certainly does,' Sally agreed. They'd
just reached an exciting part of the
Charles Dickens story, 'Hard Times',
and she was desperate to know if one of
the main characters, Sissy, decided to
continue with her education or return
to the circus. She had to admit that this
project with Bess was taking her mind
off her broken heart, too.

Helping Bess to write passages herself
proved more challenging as she lacked
a lot of confidence in this area. They
started with the spellings of basic words.

'Why is meat as in food spelt differently

to meet as in meet up?' Bess puzzled as they worked.

'I couldn't tell you.' Sally giggled. 'English is funny like that.'

'And why are there so many letters in dough? Shouldn't it be written dow?'

'I don't know!' Sally laughed.

Over the next few weeks, they found many more exceptions in the English language. Sally tried to teach Bess the rule 'i before e, except after c,'one night before bed, the scullery maid instantly pointed out that 'weight' is a notable exception.

'So's 'eight' come to think of it,' Sally said. She suddenly felt very tired and confused. 'Perhaps the only rule is that there aren't any rules. Now. Shall we go to bed?'

'But I want to get it right,' Bess said stubbornly as she painstaking copied out some text from an open book.

'You've come on leaps and bounds,' Sally encouraged her. 'Plus, you don't have to get things right all the time. Keep practising and you'll get there.'

Bess nodded but she didn't look convinced.

'What's brought this on, anyway?' Sally asked. 'Why are you so interested in reading and writing all of a sudden?

'Don't know,' Bess replied quickly with a shrug. 'Actually, it is pretty late, isn't it? We best get to bed.'

As Sally bid Bess good night and made her way back to her own bedroom where she knew Clare would have long been asleep, Sally couldn't help but feel that there was something the scullery maid wasn't telling her.

Shocking Glimpse

'Have you got a new best friend now, Sal?' Clare asked the following morning as the two girls rose for their early chores. Her tone was light but Sally could tell from the slightly pinched look on her face that her friend was slightly hurt.

'Oh, give over, course not,' Sally replied as she splashed cold water on her face and rubbed her eyes. The late nights were taking their toll and she felt exhausted, which was far from a good start to the day. 'I'm just helping her improve on her letters. It's nice to see her coming out of her shell a bit.'

'I feel like I've hardly spoken to you since you started this teaching project, Sal,' Clare said, shrugging. 'And your hair will be as knotty as a fishnet without my help.'

'Don't you worry, Clare,' Sally said, reaching out for a moment to squeeze her friend's hand. 'You'll always be my best friend. I'd be lost without our chats and your help with my hair.

'I won't be helping Bess tonight anyway. I came to bed far too late last night and I need a break.'

'That's good, Sal,' Clare replied, squeezing her hand back and looking somewhat reassured. 'Now, we'd best be off to work.'

Sally's first chore of the day consisted of cleaning out the fire grates as usual and laying down fresh coal.

The sunbeams peeped through the Hall windows as she worked. It was late April now and the weather had turned pleasant again. Once summer arrived, there'd be less need for a lit fire in every room of the house, which was always a relief for the servants.

As she swept the ash and embers into her bucket, Sally couldn't help but feel a stab of guilt over Clare's remarks that morning. The last thing she'd ever want was to hurt her best friend.

Clare wasn't as lucky as Sally when it came to family. She'd never known her father as he'd passed away whilst her mother, Joan, was expecting her. Joan had never remarried so she brought Clare up alone. The two of them had lived further down the valley towards Halifax.

Joan fell ill and passed away when Clare was only fifteen, giving her no other option than to look for work in service. Sally knew she was the closest thing Clare had to a family of her own and tried to include her friend as much as possible in the Halfpennys' life. Clare was always welcome at their cottage.

Sally sighed. Her care for others was built into her bones but there were times when it was just impossible to please everyone. Occasionally she couldn't help but wish she was more like Nancy who instinctively looked after herself, but that wasn't, and never would be, part of her nature.

The next task was to polish all the household mirrors. One glance at her reflection in the first one she came to confirmed her resolution to go to bed on time that evening. Her skin looked sallow and those dark circles that formed under her eyes every time she was over-tired were back.

Sally was glad when it was finally time to sit down for breakfast. The cook and the housekeeper were nowhere to be seen. Sally assumed they must be looking over the household accounts. Mr Sykes was reading the newspaper with his cup of coffee. He wasn't one for long conversations, especially not in the mornings.

'Gosh, you look exhausted, Sally,' Nancy commented as Sally joined the rest of the servants downstairs. 'Your cap's a little wonky, too.'

'Yes, I need more sleep,' Sally answered, straightening her cap and feeling slightly annoyed.

It was just like Nancy to point out her flaws rather than subtly bringing them to her attention when no-one else was listening. It was almost as if Nancy knew how she felt about James. Sally hoped she wasn't that transparent. Other than Clare, she didn't speak of her feelings to anyone.

'I didn't sleep a wink last night, either,'

Nancy went on. Sally found this hard to believe as the lady's maid was as neatly turned out as always and her skin was glowing with a peachy hue.

'It hit me all over again that I've most likely lost my brooch for good,' Nancy explained. 'Not to mention that lovely ribbon.' Her doe eyes filled with tears. Only Nancy could look beautiful when she cried.

'I don't suppose you'll find them now,' came a voice. Bess had come in from the kitchen to clear away some of the breakfast crockery.

'How do you know?' Nancy asked abruptly, narrowing her eyes and brushing a couple of tears away. Bess shrugged as she gathered up the plates and bowls from the table.

As she returned to the kitchen, Nancy gave a sharp gasp and her hand flew to her chest. The servants all followed her gaze. It was instantly clear what had shocked her, for just peeping out of the back of Bess's cap, was an unmistakeable flash of buttercup yellow.

It was clear to everyone in the room that the scullery maid was wearing a very nice ribbon in her hair, uncannily similar to the one Nancy had lost.

Suspicion Rises Again

'Bess,' Nancy called after her. Her voice sounded strangely high-pitched and a little shrill. She'd risen from her chair at the table and was now standing with one hand on her hip. Her whole body was rigid and the air felt tight with unease. Sally had never seen Nancy look so tense before.

'Yes?' Bess reappeared at the door and leaned slightly on the frame. She looked supremely relaxed by comparison.

'Are you wearing a yellow ribbon in your hair?'

'That's right.' Bess still didn't look in any way worried. She removed her cap for a moment and, turning around, shook her head a little, to display the good quality ribbon wrapped into her bun. Sally had to admit that it utterly transformed her otherwise mousy brown hair. With this new-found confidence, Bess looked like a completely different young woman.

'Can I ask where you got it from?' Nancy asked. She was still standing perfectly still.

'It was a gift,' Bess replied, shrugging. She put her cap back on and then disappeared back into the kitchen.

'Not so fast,' Nancy said. Rediscovering the movement in her limbs, she rushed into the kitchen to confront the scullery maid.

'Wait,' Sally cautioned, but Nancy wasn't listening. Quickly Sally followed her. She didn't trust either of them to stay civil.

She was glad of Mrs Ackroyd's absence but wished Mrs Hartley was there. Mr Sykes was still reading the newspaper and didn't appear to be worried by the exchange. Either that or he simply didn't wish to be involved.

It wasn't long before James had joined them in the kitchen. Sally could tell by the look on his face that he was just as uncomfortable as she was.

'A gift from whom?' Nancy asked, folding her arms. Bess turned from the vegetables she was chopping and met Nancy's gaze.

'That's my business, thank you very much,' she said evenly.

'Well, I'd say it's my business too, given I've lost a ribbon that's identical to that one in your hair,' Nancy answered in a flash. Her voice was still high-pitched and Sally could tell that her temper was fraying.

'You're not the only girl in the world who owns a pretty ribbon, Nancy,' Bess answered. If she did feel worried by another accusation, she certainly wasn't letting it show. 'Perhaps you should take better care of your things.'

Nancy's face crumpled at that and she fled out of the kitchen and through the servants' dining-room.

'You haven't heard the last of this, Bess Trimble,' she yelled before storming up the stairs in a fit of sobs.

The remaining servants stood awkwardly in her wake. Mr Sykes finally looked up from his newspaper.

'Girls, girls,' he murmured before

rising to refill his cup. Sally waited to see if he'd say anything else but he didn't and returned to the paper once his coffee was replenished.

'I'll speak to Mrs Hartley,' he muttered eventually, when he realised Sally was looking at him. Amidst raised eyebrows and hurried whispers, the servants left the dining-room to get back to work. It didn't look like the mystery would be solved any time soon.

★ ★ ★

Despite Sally's best efforts to focus on her duties for the rest of the day, her mind kept returning to the unfortunate exchange that morning.

A feeling was gnawing away at the back of her brain and, against her better judgement, she couldn't stop herself approaching Bess after finishing her evening meal. She'd seen neither Nancy nor James since breakfast that morning.

'Bess, can I have a quick word?'

'What is it, Sal?' The scullery maid

was attending to the pots as usual as they steamed and bubbled away. Sally placed a cup of tea on the work surface. She'd made it with plenty of milk and sugar, just the way Bess liked it.

'About that yellow ribbon.'

'I didn't take it.'

Sally saw that the bright yellow fabric was still peeping out of Bess's cap.

'No, I don't believe you did,' Sally answered carefully, 'but can't you tell me who gave it to you, Bess? It might help clear your name.'

'It was a friend, Sal, and that's all I'm saying,' Bess answered shortly. 'Please don't ask me anything more as I've nowt to tell you.'

'Fair enough, Bess,' Sally replied, sensing that she was beaten. 'Remember where I am if you ever want to talk.'

★ ★ ★

'It's so frustrating,' Sally remarked to Clare as they got ready for bed later that evening. She'd kept to her word and hadn't offered to help Bess with her studies tonight and Clare had just finished attacking her knotty locks with the brush. In the light of the day's events, it was quite a relief to have a night off.

'I'm trying to help her, but she won't open up to me.'

'I've told you before, Sal, that lass does nowt to help herself,' Clare said as she climbed on to her bed and lay back on the pillow.

'I was just thinking that she'd finally settled in here and started to blossom,' Sally went on. 'I fear she's taken several steps backwards now.'

'What do you think happened to the ribbon, Sal?' Clare asked as Sally splashed water on her face and then climbed into her bed.

'I don't know yet, but I have my suspicions,' Sally replied. 'I'll tell you about them later, once I have more proof.'

'It's May Day soon,' Clare said dreamily. 'That'll surely put everyone in a better mood.'

'Oh, yes, it always does,' Sally replied.

It felt good to be back to normal with her closest friend at the Hall. As much as she enjoyed tutoring Bess, she had to admit that there was no way the younger girl would ever replace the friendship she had with Clare. The bond between the housemaids wasn't something she'd ever want to jeopardise. Realising that she was feeling tired, Sally felt her eyes close and her body sink into the sheets.

Soon happy thoughts of the annual spring time celebrations were winging their way through her head and it wasn't long before she fell into a deep and much-needed sleep.

★ ★ ★

'Good to see you, our Sal!' Mary Halfpenny called from the sunken myrtle green armchair when her husband flung the door open to welcome Sally indoors.

It was a Saturday afternoon a couple of days later and Sally was happy to have a few hours off to visit her family.

The mid-spring sun had shone warmly

on her face as she'd walked over from the Hall and it was such a relief to feel the tension from the last few days at the Hall all but disappear into the gentle breeze.

Bluebells carpeted the waysides and the hawthorn trees were laden with blossoms. The tiny delicate flowers danced in the air and fell to the ground like a rose-tinted snowfall.

'Hello, all.' Sally grinned as she entered the kitchen. The kettle was whistling and her father was already holding her blue bird cup in his hand ready to fill.

'Goodness, are you feeling all right, Pa?' Sally asked with a smile as she sat down on one of the wooden chairs at the kitchen table. 'Ma is sitting in your chair and you're the one making tea.'

'I'm feeling fine, Sal,' Fred replied. 'It's Ma who's not feeling right. That's why she's having a rest.'

'Oh no — what's wrong?' Sally's smile evaporated into the air like the steam from the boiling kettle.

'I'm just not feeling myself, Sal,' Mary answered with a sigh. 'Your pa's making a right fuss of me, but really, you mustn't worry.'

'I always worry, Ma,' Sally answered, fearing already that the fever had returned to Brackenfold.

'I don't feel hot, lovey,' Mary assured her. 'More tired and my joints are aching.'

'Perhaps you're just getting old, Ma,' came a voice. William had appeared at the kitchen door.

'Will!' Sally scolded, but her parents smiled good-naturedly.

'I hope that's all it is, our Will.' Mary laughed. 'Now, Sal, give us all the news from the Hall to distract me from my ageing limbs. I've heard Nancy's had some things go missing. People seem to think there's some thievery afoot.'

Sally took a deep breath and told her family all about the accusations, the enigmatic Mr Crookshanks and her own worries for the wellbeing of Bess.

'It's all a bit of a mess,' she concluded as she sipped her tea and gratefully tucked into the bread and dripping her father had set beside her.

'It certainly is, Sal,' Mary agreed as she sat back in the chair. 'Hopefully May Day will bring everyone together and put all this nonsense to bed.'

'Oh, yes,' Sally answered and soon the whole family were chatting excitedly about the upcoming celebrations which were only a week away.

May Day had been observed by the folk of Brackenfold valley ever since anyone could remember. Mrs Hartley said once that it dated back to ancient times and was a celebration of new life and fertility.

For the villagers, however, it was an excuse to forget about work for a day and come together for some revelry and fun, as well as welcoming in the warmer weather as summertime approached. The mills all closed for the day and those in service were given a day off as well.

'May Day is my favourite festival,' Sally mused as the family continued to chat about it. 'I even prefer it to Christmas. I think it's because it's a chance for us all to get together, regardless of our age or station. Normal rules don't apply!'

'Too true, our Sal,' Mary agreed. She was still sitting back in her chair and had closed her eyes now.

Sally continued to joke and laugh with her father and brother, but inside she couldn't help but acknowledge that her mother was looking so tired these days. There were fine lines all over her face now and her skin looked thinner somehow, as if it would crumple any second, like the fine paper the older Mr Fairclough used for his letters.

As Sally bid her family farewell and made her way back across the valley to the Hall, a curious feeling she couldn't quite name washed over her and, try as she might, she couldn't shake it off for the rest of the day.

That night, as she tried to sleep, she found her dreams were littered with images of her mother being pulled away by a rushing deep river whilst Sally stood helpless on the bank and screamed into the darkness.

May Day Arrives

Sally woke on May Day morning to the sound of Clare calling her name and tugging at her bedsheets.

'Quickly, Sal, wake up! It's nearly dawn!' It was the tradition to rise before sunrise on May Day and to wash one's face in the morning dew.

With their servants' habits, the former custom was considerably easier to achieve than the latter, and they made do with splashing their faces with water from their bedroom jug instead and sniffing the fresh forget-me-nots and cowslips that the gardener had begrudgingly allowed them to pick from the Hall grounds the previous day.

Gathering flowers was another May Day tradition which the people of Brackenfold liked to keep going. They had used some of them to create floral garlands the evening before which they'd wear on their heads and round their necks.

Another of the May Day customs they

liked to observe was for all the young and unmarried women in the village to wear white for the festival.

Clare was keen to get straight out to the village but Sally reminded her that they'd better eat some breakfast first. She was tired and in need of the nourishment.

Sally had continued to help Bess with her letters on some of the evenings that week, but since the argument with Nancy, Bess had become rather reclusive again and seemed to have lost some of her enthusiasm for learning.

Sally wanted to talk with her about it again but it was hard to find the time when everyone was so busy. They'd worked extra hard over the past week to ensure they were fully up to date with all their tasks to allow for the holiday.

Mrs Ackroyd had prepared a cold self-serve breakfast for the family to eat before they joined in with the festivities as well.

The Faircloughs enjoyed May Day as much as the regular folk of Brackenfold, as did all the higher echelons of society. Part of the magic of May Day was the bringing together of everyone in the community. It was one of the precious few days of the year when money and status were forgotten.

Well, almost forgotten, Sally thought to herself wryly, as she found the white flowing dress she always wore for May Day at the back of her wardrobe. Every year a May Queen was selected to lead the village parade in a sedan chair covered in spring flowers. She represented the Roman Goddess, Flora, who was generally regarded as the personification of spring. According to tradition, the girl deemed the most beautiful in the village would be chosen for May Queen.

Sally was fairly sure that a different girl was supposed to be chosen each time. In Brackenfold, however, the role had been given to Miss Amelia Fairclough every year since she was ten years old. It was something the other girls of the village had grown to accept, along with all the other inequalities of life.

Miss Amelia had a new white silken gown specially made each year for the celebration, each one more flamboyant and eye-catching than the last.

The finer details of the dress were a closely guarded secret each year until the day itself, though Nancy had whispered that this year, the gown was covered in silk roses dusted in precious stones. Clearly no expense was to be spared in the pursuit of the perfect frock.

'She'll have run out of ideas of what to wear by the time she's wed,' Mrs Ackroyd had said, rolling her eyes. 'If that day ever comes,' she'd added under her breath.

'Right, Sal, ready for a quick breakfast?' Clare asked, breaking into Sally's thoughts.

'Absolutely,' she answered. 'Goodness, Clare, you look stunning!' Sally had been so lost in her own thoughts that she'd barely noticed her friend getting ready.

With her glossy dark hair and her flawless pale skin, Clare had always struck Sally as very pretty, but amidst the drudgery and toil of their everyday lives, she'd never fully appreciated the true extent of Clare's beauty until now. Clare wasn't one to show it off like Nancy and was usually quite shy in big groups.

Sally noticed how the white of Clare's simple gown brought out the gentle rose-pink in her cheeks and the garland of cowslips resting lightly in her raven hair gave her the look of a goddess from the ancient world. Her eyes looked wider and bluer, somehow.

'Ah, thanks, lovey,' Clare answered, giggling. 'Now, come on you, or we'll miss the parade.'

Arm in arm the two housemaids left the Hall along with the other servants, following a swift breakfast.

Mercifully, the weather had been kind to them and Sally enjoyed the feeling of the morning sun smiling warmly down on them as they made their way along the gravelly stone paths to the village green to meet up with the other revellers.

Sally wondered if she should invite Bess to walk with them. The scullery maid, however, had set off at quite a determined pace and was a few yards ahead of the group.

Sally had tried to give Bess a garland for her head, but she'd declined and her hair was tucked up in the straw hat she always wore for church on Sundays, though she was at least wearing a white dress with a sprig of pink apple blossom pinned to the front.

Sally sincerely hoped that bright yellow ribbon, which had already caused Bess so many problems, wasn't hiding under her hat, too. It wouldn't do to ignite Nancy's anger and spoil what should be a pleasant holiday for everyone.

Sally's thoughts soon turned to other matters. She couldn't help but notice that James and Nancy were following their fellow servants at a slight distance from the main group.

They weren't far enough behind to cause any raised eyebrows or disapproving remarks, but to Sally, James might as well have been several seas away.

She tried not to notice how fresh and lovely Nancy looked in her own white gown and garland. The white set off her honeyblonde hair to perfection and her skin looked as if she'd caught the sun slightly.

James also looked well turned-out in his best beige trousers and blue checked shirt with braces. Somehow the sting of Sally's unrequited love never got easier to bear. She swallowed hard and clung to Clare's arm.

'Morning!'

'May Day blessings.'

'Right nice day for it.'

The greetings came thick and fast as the servants of the Hall raised their hands and exchanged excited pleasantries with the villagers. It wasn't long before everyone from housewives to mill workers had joined them on their way to the festivities.

'Oh!' Clare gave a little squeal and Sally felt a sharp tug on her arm as Clare stumbled on what appeared to be a wooden spinning top. For a stomach-dropping moment, Sally thought they were both going to fall into the dirt and gravel of the path, but somehow she managed to keep steady and Clare merely wobbled for a few moments before taking a few deep breaths and coming to a standstill.

'Timothy!' an angry voice shouted and before the girls knew it, a red-faced young man in brown striped trousers and a white shirt had rushed over. 'I told you not to bring that daft top of yours,' he went on, picking up the toy from the path and handing it to a bright-eyed and cheeky-faced youngster who'd run over too.

'I do apologise, ladies,' the young man said eventually.

His face was still flushed and he seemed to find it hard to meet their eyes. Sally subtly took note of his fine light brown hair and the strong muscles underneath his shirt.

One look at Clare told Sally that her friend had noticed them, too. She was self-consciously checking that her garland was sitting straight on her head and seemed quite flustered.

'No harm done,' Sally said eventually, sensing that Clare would rather she do the talking. 'He's just excited, like the rest of us.'

'Thank you for being so understanding,' the young man replied with a grateful grin. His skin was returning to normal and the smile transformed his face into one that was more than a little bit handsome. The young lad had scampered off, presumably back to the rest of the family.

'My little brother doesn't understand the word no.'

'I was the same when I was a girl.' Clare spoke up, having found her voice at last. 'My poor ma was run ragged with me.'

'Our Tim will drive us all to an early grave, but we can't help but love him!' The young man seemed much more comfortable now. 'I'm Adam Shaw,' he continued.

As the girls introduced themselves in return, the three of them continued on their way.

The other servants were quite far ahead of them now, though Mrs Hartley had lingered to check that all was well. She walked a little further ahead though turned slightly every so often, to check they weren't lagging too far behind.

'My family have been sheep farming in the south Pennines for years,' Adam explained as they walked.

'Ah, yes, I've heard of your family up at Rugged Royd Farm,' Sally remarked. She'd heard her father mention them from time to time.

Living up in the blustery and desolate hills was a hard existence but the Shaws were known to be hardy folk. They refused to be tempted down the valley sides and stayed true to their roots, despite the difficulties farmers faced these days.

Sally's father always spoke highly of the Shaws and said if anyone could make it up there, it was them. They wove their own cloth from the sheep's wool as well as selling lamb and mutton to folk in the valley villages and towns.

'One day we hope to buy back the land from our landlords the Faircloughs,' Adam was saying. 'It's been our family's aim for years.'

'I hope you do,' Sally replied. It sometimes felt as if the Faircloughs' realm reached every corner of the West Riding.

They were decent people, of course, but it would be nice if some more ordinary folk were given the opportunity to own the land on which they worked and make something of themselves.

'We've all been looking forward to May Day,' Adam went on. 'Our grandpa refuses to leave the flock each year, but insists we all come down for a rare family day out.'

'The time off is very welcome,' Sally agreed as she explained that she and Clare worked at the Hall.

The girls were just in the middle of telling Adam of all the ups and downs of servant life, and, in a slightly hushed tone, the joys of working with characters like Mrs Ackroyd, when they were silenced by several loud beats of a drum and a fanfare of trumpets.

Once they'd turned a corner and were on the village green, Sally let out a squeal of delight. It happened every year but still, she always forgot how the May Day celebrations transformed the small valley village into a springtime wonderland which simply bubbled with magic and delight.

The band had set themselves up in the centre of the green and it wasn't long before the lilting notes of the fiddle had joined the May Day music.

Directly beside the band was the maypole itself. They'd used a fir tree trunk, with all the branches taken off. A rainbow of silken ribbons had been wrapped round the top, ready for dancing later. Villagers had placed bunting and streamers on their front doors and gates adding to the festival atmosphere.

There were plenty of stalls selling refreshments. Sally caught the sweet sugary scents of candyfloss and melted chocolate as they floated over in the gentle morning breeze.

There was savoury food on offer, too, like cups of pea soup, hot pies, sizzling sausages in teacakes and baked potatoes oozing with salty butter.

The green was dotted with games, for adults and children alike, offering real prizes like wooden trains, toy soldiers and shiny tin whistles. There was croquet, lawn bowls, hoopla and even an archery tournament.

Young girls in white gowns and floral garlands floated around like angels, giving an otherworldly effect to the whole place.

Sally squeezed Clare's arm, feeling certain she'd be just as enchanted. When she turned to look at her best friend, however, she saw that rather than staring at the May Day spectacle, Clare was smiling shyly into Adam's grey eyes. He was looking at her directly now and something told Sally that Clare would hold his gaze for ever.

Romance Blossoms

The servants of Brackenfold quickly dispersed into the crowd once they reached the village green, though Sally noticed that Mrs Hartley stayed relatively close by.

'Our Sal!'

Sally looked up to see her parents on the other side of the green. William was bound to be around somewhere close by with his mates from the mill, too.

She looked at Clare who was listening intently to something Adam was saying about lambing. Would it be improper to leave them alone unchaperoned?

She was beginning to feel rather like an unwanted guest at a private party, but she couldn't risk Clare's reputation being spoiled, especially as they were at an event attended by the whole community. Sally knew how quickly word spread in a small place like Brackenfold.

She took a look at Mrs Hartley who was still standing fairly near to them and caught the housekeeper's eye. In a split second, Mrs Hartley gave Sally a subtle but definitive nod of her head, which Sally took as permission to slip off quietly, safe in the knowledge that the older woman would keep a watchful eye over her friend.

With a grateful smile, Sally took her leave. She wasn't sure Clare even noticed.

'Ma,' she cried, clasping her mother's hand when she reached them, 'how are you feeling?'

'I'm doing all right, thanks, Sal,' Mary replied, though Sally didn't feel hugely convinced. Her mother's smile was bright but her face looked paler than ever. Fred looked tired and worried, as well.

'Perhaps you should take her home,' Sally suggested to him.

'I tried but she'll have none of it,' Fred answered, shrugging. 'I can't get her to take any more time off work, either.'

'Ma,' Sally began, placing a hand on her hips and trying to look stern.

'Give over! Both of you!' It was Mary's turn to look cross. 'It's May Day, for crying out loud, and we're here to have a day off from our woes and concerns. I've come here to have fun and I insist that you do, too.'

'Well, at least sit down on this bench,' Sally said after exchanging a glance with her father. 'We'll get a good view from there.'

Thankfully, Mary agreed to the compromise and soon the three of them were sitting down with a cold bottle of ginger beer each.

Sally tried to keep a look out for Clare. Her friend normally joined the Halfpennys at village festivals like this and it felt rather strange without her. Soon, however, Sally became distracted by the sights and sounds of the May Day festivities.

'Oh, my goodness, I think that's Mr Julian.' Sally giggled, as a figure resembling an evergreen shrub emerged from one of the grand Fairclough carriages. He was wearing a wicker frame that was entwined with all manner of green foliage and a garland of leaves had been placed on his head.

Like his father before him, Mr Julian Fairclough had taken on the role of 'Jack in the Green' every year since he'd reached adulthood. It was the one time of the year that he dropped his serious façade and relaxed with the rest of the village.

No-one was quite sure of the true origin of the tradition of Jack in the Green. Some said he emerged from the custom of making May Day garlands and that some youngsters had become over-excited one year and covered one of their friends entirely in foliage, thus starting the custom of a 'green man'.

But then, Sally remembered her father telling her once that Jack in the Green was often associated with chimney sweeps. As May Day was one of the few holidays granted to them, it was thought that the sweeps covered themselves in extra-large garlands during the May Day parades in the hopes they'd get larger donations from the crowd who'd hand out pennies to those in costume, and that, over time, the character had emerged from this custom.

Whatever Jack's source, it was nice to see her master embracing the role so enthusiastically. She couldn't imagine May Day without the laughing green figure who was loved by all the community.

Sally and her parents watched as Mr Julian began walking round the stalls waving at the villagers, especially small children who watched him in awe. His own daughter, Miss Florence, wore a tiny garland and a snow-white frock with little satin flowers sewn in, presumably to mirror her Auntie Amelia's May Queen outfit, as perhaps the May Princess.

It wasn't long before the toddler was charging around like a miniature packhorse whilst poor Rachel tried in vain to keep her under control.

As Miss Florence stumbled and then toppled face down into the grass, Sally felt pretty certain that it wouldn't be long before the little girl would more closely resemble her father's character than that of her elegant aunt. Green Baby felt more apt than May Princess.

Sally knew that Miss Amelia would make her grand arrival soon, which signified the start of the May Day parade. Sally would then join the other young women of Brackenfold to walk alongside the sedan chair as they circulated the green and a few surrounding streets.

She scanned the crowd again for Clare and eventually spied her sitting with Adam on the other side of the green. He had bought them both some candyfloss.

Mrs Hartley stood with Mrs Ackroyd several paces away, which Sally found reassuring and anyway, no-one appeared to be paying the young pair any particular attention. After all, May Day was a time where the normal rules of society didn't necessarily apply.

Still, Sally hoped with all her being that this exciting development for her friend lasted a lot longer than this short-lived holiday. She wouldn't wish her lovelorn state on anyone, let alone her best friend.

Sally looked around for other familiar figures. Mr Sykes and a few of the stable lads were having a go at the hoopla, whilst James was buying Nancy some lemonade at one of the stalls.

Sally felt some unwelcome envy stirring in her chest. She would have given anything to spend May Day with James. Something about the way Nancy was idly blowing a dandelion clock as she waited for her drink told Sally that she remained fairly unappreciative of his efforts.

Sally distracted herself by looking for Bess instead but the scullery maid was nowhere to be seen.

'All right, Sal,' came a voice and Sally looked round to see William approaching with a group of his friends from the mill. Like the other villagers, they were well turned out in their good clothes.

'You're looking quite smart today, Will!' Sally didn't bother to hide her surprise. She generally saw her older brother in his grubby work overalls and it had given her quite a start to see him in best brown trousers and striped shirt with braces. His hair, which was dark and curly, like hers, sat quite neatly under his grey flat cap.

'I try and scrub up once a year,' he replied. 'You're looking very nice yourself, Sal.'

'Goodness, are you two feeling quite well?' Mary laughed. 'I'm the one who's supposed to be poorly, remember!'

'Don't worry, Ma. We'll be squabbling again before long.' William laughed. 'Right, we're off to have a go at the hoopla. I'm determined to win one of those nice bright tin whistles this year.'

'Why?' Sally laughed as William and his friends dispersed. 'You've never played a musical instrument in your life!'

'First time for everything, Sal!' William shouted back in reply as he ran off.

A few moments later, Sally heard a clatter of hooves on the cobbled road and looked up to see the rich oak of another of the Faircloughs' carriages approaching, complete with the golden eagle and white stag of their family crest.

'She's here.' Sally nudged her mother. A crowd of people had formed round the carriage as soon as it came to a standstill by the green. The Halfpennys stood up to try and get a better view.

'She's a bonnie one, that's for sure,' Mary murmured as they took in Miss Amelia's long flowing silken gown, with its delicately laced bodice and pretty cap sleeves.

Nancy had been right; the dress was dotted with fine silk flowers which were decorated in sparkling jewels. Diamonds, most likely, Sally guessed. With a garland of violets sitting on her blonde hair, Miss Amelia was a true spring queen. She was utterly captivating. Sally found it hard to look away.

'Go on then, Sal, stop gawping,' Mary said eventually, giving her daughter a light prod in the back. The sedan chair had arrived too and, having waved graciously at the crowd for a minute or two and accepted a couple of posies of flowers from villagers near the carriage, Miss Amelia was now settling herself down on her seat, ready for the May Day parade.

Waving a quick goodbye to her parents, Sally ran along the green to join the rest of the young women as they walked behind the queen.

'Sal, over here!' Clare waved enthusiastically from towards the back of the group of girls that had formed around the chair.

'You've managed to tear yourself away from him, then?' Sally giggled as she joined her friend and squeezed her arm.

'Oh, Sal, this must be a dream,' Clare replied. Her arm was shaking slightly and she couldn't keep still. 'He's the best fella I've ever met!'

'I'm happy for you, lovey,' Sally answered, squeezing her friend's arm again.

'But I'm scared of folk talking,' Clare went on. 'What if word spreads that I'm, you know, the wrong kind of woman?' Her words were quick and fearful.

'Anyone who knows you will think nothing of the sort, Clare,' Sally replied. 'We've only just met Adam, I know, but he seems decent and I'm sure his intentions are honourable. Just don't disappear with him and stay in the crowds, then no-one will have owt to say.'

Clare nodded and squeezed Sally's arm in return.

The group was beginning to move. Sally had a quick look around. Nancy and Ellie were in front of them and were chatting to some girls from the mill. There was still no sign of Bess.

She could see Adam standing with his younger brother, Tim, and a few others whom she guessed were the rest of his family. He still couldn't take his eyes off Clare.

James was standing by and appeared to be talking to Mr Sykes, but Sally noticed that he kept taking sideways glances at Nancy. Sally took a deep breath, and tried not to care that there was no young man looking out for her. She smiled at no-one in particular and despite the hard tug of her wounded heart, tried her best to make the most of the May Day holiday.

Night Falls

The May Day procession circled the village green twice before making a short tour of the surrounding streets. Older folk and those who were unwell, so unable to come to the main event, would come to their front doors with a smile and a wave as the young women walked by.

Some had hung bunting from their front doors or filled clay pots with flowers for the occasion. Clare talked about Adam nonstop and whilst Sally remained pleased for her friend, she found it quite hard to keep her envy at bay.

'He's so funny, Sal. He had me laughing for a whole ten minutes when he told me about Gertie, his pet pig. She's ever so bad tempered, you know.'

Sally laughed good-naturedly as the procession turned a corner and passed by some poorer houses in the village.

'Oh, Clare, I do feel sorry for the poor souls who have to live here.'

'Isn't it miserable, Sal,' Clare agreed.

Sally was glad of a change of topic and turned her attention to the houses, which were little more than terraced shacks and were all in need of repair.

The Faircloughs generally ensured that their millworkers lived in homes owned by themselves, which were all reasonably well maintained, if not exactly luxurious. Other landlords, however, weren't nearly as responsible and took little or no interest in the welfare of their tenants.

Sally noticed that the roofs were falling apart and that some of the window panes didn't even have any glass in them. The wood on many of the front doors was rotting too and there was an unpleasant smell of leaking sewage in the warm air.

Sally noticed that Miss Amelia had raised a dainty pink pocket handkerchief to her nose and wondered if she might do the same. She focused on the sweet smell of her garland of flowers instead, as she didn't want people thinking she had ideas beyond her station.

Before long, Sally noticed two young women emerge from one of the houses. She saw the white of Bess's frock before she recognised the scullery maid. It was stark against the grubby soot-stained stone of the terrace. Bess had removed her hat and thankfully there was no sign of the contentious yellow ribbon in her hair.

She smiled as she recognised Sally and Clare in the crowd. Sally was about to beckon her to come and join them but then thought better of it.

The other girl, who had to be Meg, the sister Bess spoke of sometimes, was wearing in a shabby grey dress, parts of which had clearly been mended several times. Meg's dark eyes resembled Bess's and she had the same mousy brown hair. There was a pinched look to her cheeks that spoke of poverty and need.

Sally noticed how closely the two girls stood together. When Bess whispered something into her sister's ear, Meg's face transformed into a lovely warm smile which almost erased that pinched look altogether.

As they walked past their house, Sally peeped into the front room window, which thankfully retained its glass, though it was thick with dust and grime. She caught a quick glimpse of a wan and sad-looking face peering out at the procession and quickly turned away. She was glad when they left that part of the village.

The May Day celebrations continued once the parade was over. Miss Amelia circulated the green on foot and happily accepted more posies from the villagers as she soaked up all their attention.

The sun was high in the sky now as the afternoon approached.

Sally's parents stayed for a short while longer before telling her that they'd decided to retire back to their cottage for the rest of the afternoon, so Mary could have a lie down.

Sally thought she could see more worry stirring behind her father's eyes but said nothing more. She had a feeling that voicing her concerns any more than she had already would do nothing to help the situation. She looked around for William but he was nowhere to be seen.

'Sal, come over here with us,' Clare called from further up the green. She had lost no time in joining Adam again but they were with the rest of his family now, too.

Feeling less like a gooseberry, Sally gratefully walked over to see them. She wasn't sure who she could spend time with otherwise and a festival like this was hardly a day to be by yourself.

The Shaws were all eating pies and jacket potatoes bought from the stall holders washed down with a few bottles of lemonade. They quickly handed a generous portion over to Sally and waved away her offer of a penny to pay them back.

Clare shared her bottle of lemonade with Sally, too. The refreshment was very welcome. Sally hadn't realised it until she took her first bite of pie, but she really was quite hungry.

A group of Morris Dancers had formed around the band and it wasn't long before they were performing energetic and entertaining sets to the jolly notes of the fiddle and quite a crowd gathered to watch.

The dancers were all in white, with bright red caps on their heads. Tiny bells were strapped to their ankles and rang out in time to the music. They waved white handkerchiefs as they danced and some held smooth wooden sticks.

Sally always enjoyed watching them and was glad the tradition was still alive in the village. Little Tim and a couple more of Adam's younger brothers tried to emulate the steps and had everyone in stitches, especially when they tripped over their own feet. It would seem that the next generation were keen to keep the tradition going.

Once the Morris dancers had finished, the children of Brackenfold schoolhouse formed round the maypole ready to dance for the crowd. The band continued to play and soon a mass of vibrantly coloured silk ribbons flew through the sky as the children danced in formation creating intricate weaves with the ribbons as they did so.

Sally thought back to her own childhood when she too had danced round the pole. She had always tried to pick a yellow ribbon. The sunny colour reminded her of the buttercups and dandelions on the village green and in the valleys surrounding Brackenfold.

Now, of course, yellow ribbons made her think of the suspicion and tension back home at the Hall. She'd give anything to go back to the simplicity of her all-too-fleeting childhood now. She'd never heard of heartbreak or thievery back then.

Adam continued to talk non-stop to Clare. Sally heard her laugh ring out several times and, once again, felt rather wistful about her own loveless state.

Still, thoughts of the shabby little house where Bess and her family lived sent sharp stabs of guilt right through her. Mary had told her once that there will always be folk better off than you and there'll always be those worse off, too. Sally had never fully appreciated the truth of those words until now.

She resolved to be even kinder to Bess and perhaps slip her some of her own food, if she could get away with it, which the scullery maid might take home to her mother and Meg.

As the lowest in the servants' hierarchy, Bess was always given the most meagre of portions and Mrs Ackroyd was well known for keeping a close eye on all the food in her kitchen, down to the last crusts of bread.

Bess couldn't pilfer any provisions even if she wanted to.

Sally found that she couldn't get Meg's pinched hungry cheeks out of her mind. When she remembered how closely the sisters had been standing together and how Meg's face had broken into a wide smile when Bess leaned over to speak to her, Sally realised then that she needn't have wished for Bess to find a close friend like Clare after all. She had a soulmate already in her younger sister.

In what felt like no time at all, the sun had crept over to the west. Sally watched how the evening rays lit up the long grass and wild flowers at the edge of the green and lifted up her face to catch the best of the warmth.

The band were still playing their jaunty beats but the formal dancing had stopped now and parents were calling out to their younger children that it was time to go home. The games remained open and the drinks stalls began selling tankards of beer and cider, much to the delight of several of the villagers.

Sally smiled to herself as she saw Bertie Wheeler standing at the front of the queue. He worked at the mill with William and was known to enjoy a tipple or two. Sally watched as Adam's mother gathered up her smaller children, including little Tim, who was still clutching his spinning top.

'We'll stay for a while longer,' Adam said, grinning, gesturing to his older brother, his brother's wife and his two sisters. 'Are you two allowed to stay on?'

The girls nodded in reply. The Brack-enfold staff were generally permitted to remain at village events like the May Day festivities until after dark on the under-standing that their behaviour was always exemplary and that they got up for work as normal the following day.

Sally spied a couple of the stable lads queuing up for beer. It wouldn't do to drink too much. Personally, she never touched alcohol but was happy to see the others partake in a little at Christ-mas time and other special events like May Day.

As daytime turned into twilight, the lamplighter came out and soon the fes-tivities were bathed in an amber glow. Several of the villagers brought out their own lanterns as well. The air tempera-ture retained its warmth as the sky began to darken. Some couples had started to dance as the band played on.

'Good day, Sal?' came a voice. Sally looked up to see James standing in front of her. His face looked soft in the lantern light, which also caught his fair hair and gave it a golden tint. He was holding two bottles of lemonade.

'Lovely, thanks,' she replied brightly. Out of the corner of her eye, she saw Clare and Adam begin to dance with the others.

'I bought some lemonade for me and Nance, but she's over there and seems happy enough so you might as well have hers,' James said, handing Sally one of the bottles.

She couldn't hide her beam of happiness as she accepted the drink. If only James knew what the small gesture meant to her, even if she was second choice.

They both looked over to where Nancy was standing with Ellie and a couple of other girls from the Hall. Naturally, she looked more beautiful than ever in the gentle lantern light. Sally saw several of the men sending admiring glances her way. Some were more subtle than others.

Nancy and her friends were watching a group of lads take turns on the hoopla which was still going, despite the vendor shaking his head and looking at his pocket watch pointedly every few seconds.

'So close!' a familiar deep voice cried out and Sally realised that William was amongst the group of players. He was the only one of the lads who wasn't stealing glances at Nancy and was far too busy trying to win at hoopla to notice her.

'It's always right fun on May Day,' James went on. Sally wondered if he'd noticed all the attention Nancy was getting. 'I'm glad you're here actually, Sal, as there's something I wanted to ask you.'

'Oh, yes?' Sally felt an involuntary lurch in her stomach and her heart began to thump hard.

'Well, you and me are pals, aren't we, Sal? You're probably my closest friend in the Hall, truth be told.'

'Yes,' she said again. She could barely hear her voice over the pounding in her chest and the music of the band.

'Do you think I should ask Nancy to marry me?' James blurted out. 'I mean, we've had an understanding for some time now, but it's never been official, if you know what I mean.'

'If that's what you want.' Sally heard the words leave her mouth but it was as if someone else was speaking. She had thought that her heart was so broken already that it was impossible to hurt any more. She realised now that there were many miles still to go.

'But do you think she'll say yes, Sal? Do you think she'll have me?'

Sally opened her mouth to say that Nancy would be mad to turn him down, but in that moment, they were both distracted by a triumphant whoop from the hoopla and moved in a bit closer to see what was going on. It was then that they saw William punching the air and dancing on the ground in victory.

'I've done it!' he cried. 'I've won. Finally!'

'There you go,' the vendor said gruffly, handing William a shiny tin whistle. 'Right, I'm off for a beer. The game's closed.'

With that, he was gone and the crowd

began to disperse. Sally watched as William examined his prize with interest and turned it over several times in his hands.

'I'm not one for musical instruments,' he said eventually, as Sally had known all along. 'Why don't you have it?' he said impulsively to the girl standing nearest to him, who was, as it happened, none other than Nancy herself.

'Thank you!' she replied in complete surprise. As William grinned, tipped his hat and ran off into the night to rejoin his friends, Sally noticed how Nancy stared after him, as if spellbound, as she clutched the gift tight in her hands.

Back to Work

The days following the May Day celebrations felt particularly harsh and the usual drudgery of the work seemed much more draining than normal.

'It's as if we never had a break at all,' Sally commented to Clare as they got ready for bed a few nights after the holiday. 'I'm exhausted.'

'I know what you mean, Sal,' Clare replied as she sat on her bed, gazing out at the starlit sky from their tiny attic window. 'My brain has been all topsy-turvy since the May Day fun.'

'I wonder why,' Sally answered, smiling. Clare had been in a dreamy world all of her own ever since the holiday. She'd bid Adam goodbye with a squeeze of the hand whilst he promised to call by the Hall at the first opportunity.

A bunch of dusky pink roses for her had already arrived with the latest delivery from Rugged Royd Farm. They were sitting in a jam jar of water on the girls' narrow window-sill and really brightened up their bare little room.

Sally remained delighted for her friend but that hint of envy endured and was for ever lurking at the back of her mind.

How easy it had been for Clare to meet and fall in love with a fellow who returned her feelings with equal vigour. It was lucky beyond belief. But then again, Sally reasoned, Clare didn't have any family left and, until she'd met Adam, had only had Sally by way of loved ones, so really if anyone deserved a smooth and straightforward courtship, it was Clare.

'By heck, I'm right shattered,' Ellie announced at breakfast the following morning. Sally felt somewhat relieved to hear that she wasn't the only one struggling to re-adjust to their daily toil.

'It's always like this, lass,' Mrs Ackroyd replied, sprinkling brown sugar on her porridge. 'We wait all year for the holidays and they're over before you know it and you feel twice as exhausted as you did before.'

'Roll on Rushbearing,' Ellie murmured, clearly anticipating the next staff holiday.

'Don't wish your life away, lass,' Mrs Ackroyd answered sourly as she stirred her porridge. 'The likes of us needn't waste much time dreaming. Our lives are nowt really but work, and don't you forget it.'

'I feel shocking, too,' Rachel, the nursemaid, announced as she took her seat at the servants' table. 'My head is pounding and my legs are aching something chronic.'

'It'll be all that running around you do after the little madam upstairs,' Mrs Ackroyd said as she took a spoonful of porridge, which was finally at the right level of sweetness for her.

'She's a handful and no mistake,' Rachel agreed. Sally noticed that her eyes had dark circles round them. Whilst the others listened to Rachel's tales of Miss Florence's unruly behaviour, Sally managed to hide a slice of bread in her skirt pocket. She knew Bess was due an afternoon off the following day and managed to save her some sugar, too. It wasn't much but every little had to help.

'No, Sal,' Bess protested later that day when Sally subtly slipped her the package later that day. 'We're all right, me, Meg and Ma.'

'Well, just take it anyway.' Sally replied. 'Feed the bread to the ducks in the river if you don't want to eat it yourself. They're always glad of the extra food.'

'Meg right enjoys walking by the water when Ma lets us out,' Bess conceded eventually as she tucked the package into her one of her pockets. 'Thanks, Sal.'

'How are you, anyway?' Sally asked carefully. 'Do you want to get back to our reading tonight? We have a few chapters of 'Hard Times' to catch up with.'

'Yes, Sal. That would be nice.' Bess finally managed a smile before returning to her work.

Despite the long hours and aching limbs, in many ways Sally was quite glad of the daily grind. The work was a distraction from her broken heart and kept her worries for her mother at bay, too. Keeping her head down and her thoughts on the next task proved a coping mechanism.

After stories with Bess most evenings, Sally's weary body collapsed beneath the sheets and sent her into a deep, dark and mercifully dreamless sleep.

★ ★ ★

'The guest rooms are needed once more,' Mrs Hartley announced one morning a week or so later. 'I've had word from Mrs Fairclough that they're expecting company again in only a matter of days.'

'Just what we need,' Mrs Ackroyd muttered crossly, helping herself to an extra spoonful of sugar for both her tea and her porridge.

'Apparently Mr Wainscot's sent a letter to say that he's in the area for business and will call into the Hall for a few days.'

'Oh, I see,' Mrs Ackroyd said, her face brightening.

'Yes,' Mrs Hartley answering, smiling a little herself. 'I thought this news would cheer you up.'

Sally looked round the room. None of the other servants looked particularly excited at the prospect of seeing Mr Crookshanks again. Nancy was gazing into her teacup with her thoughts clearly elsewhere and James had been called to assist Mr Julian with an errand in Halifax so wasn't sitting at the table anyway.

Sally thought she could see the white of Bess's apron brush against the kitchen door and wondered if she'd heard the news, but when she looked again, it was gone.

'Now I need a volunteer to focus on the guest suite,' Mrs Hartley went on. 'I know we're all busy but I would really appreciate the extra help.'

'Me!' Sally replied into an otherwise silent room.

'Oh, thank you, Sally. I can always rely on you,' Mrs Hartley said shooting her a grateful smile.

'I'd help you, Sal, but I'm still feeling pretty bad,' Rachel said, reaching for her handkerchief for about the fourth time that morning. She hadn't touched any of her breakfast and took only the tiniest sips of tea. She looked very peaky, and her neck was swollen. 'I can barely swallow a thing,' she added. Her words came out in little more than a whisper.

'You're not well at all, lass,' Mrs Ackroyd said eyeing her sternly.

'I need to see to Miss Florence,' Rachel said weakly, standing up. As she made her way to the servants' stairs, however, she wobbled slightly and had to steady herself against the wall.

'Enough of this,' Mrs Hartley announced firmly. 'Rachel, go upstairs to bed this instant. I will ask permission to call Dr Marshall. Nancy, you'll need to look after Miss Florence for now. She knows you from the time you spent with her in Rochdale when the last bout of fever hit so I don't suppose she'll protest too much at you taking Rachel's place for now.'

'Oh, no!' Nancy cried. 'What about my duties with Miss Amelia? Surely her needs come before those of that wilful little monster, especially with Mr Wain-scot coming again.'

'You've said yourself that you don't think Miss Amelia particularly cares for him,' Mrs Hartley replied firmly. 'We'll sort something out. We're a staff force of over thirty, so we can clearly make do. Now go and see to the child. She needs you.'

'It's so unfair,' Nancy muttered, rolling her eyes, but she made her way up the stairs nevertheless.

'Oh, please don't say we have another epidemic on our hands,' Mrs Hartley said as soon as Nancy had disappeared. 'Poor Rachel has clearly caught some kind of infection, even if it isn't the fever this time. I just hope it doesn't spread.'

'Me, too,' Sally answered, thinking of her mother all over again. She had another afternoon off the next day and could only hope and pray that her mother had improved a little since she'd seen her last.

As it was midweek, she planned to call into the mill to say hello to her family quickly and then perhaps sit on the village green to wait for them to finish work.

She bid the others a swift goodbye to continue with her chores and, of course, to embark on getting the guest suites ready for Mr Wainscot. She needed all the distractions she could find today.

* * *

Sally burst into the Halfpennys' cottage the following afternoon without bothering to knock. Fred had told her when she called into the mill that Mary hadn't returned to work since May Day.

'Why didn't you tell me, Pa?' she'd cried when he gave her the news. Fred's dark eyebrows were scrunched up in what looked like a permanent frown. Sally could tell how he worried he was. With its tall smoking chimneys, Fairclough's Mill was an imposing presence at the foot of the valley sides.

'I didn't want to worry you any more than necessary, Sal,' he replied, looking more anxious than ever. 'I know what you're like when you get upset. We need to be strong right now, lass.'

'I know, Pa,' Sally replied quietly. She knew that scolding him any further would do no good at all. 'I'll go and see her now.'

'Hello, Sal,' Mary said quietly from the myrtle green armchair. Her feet were propped up on a tatty old footstall and she was wrapped in a thick patchwork quilt despite the sunny weather outside.

'Oh, Ma,' Sally whispered. Her mother looked older than ever and rather frail.

'This infection's such a bother to everyone,' Mary said sadly. 'I don't know if it's fever or something else entirely. I just wish I could shake it off and get back to normal. I can't abide sitting here like this.'

Sally murmured supportive remarks and read to her mother from 'Household Words', and when Mary grew tired, she simply sat next to her holding her hand.

'I'm going to ask the Faircloughs to call Dr Marshall out to see Ma,' Sally confided to Fred and William when they returned from their day at the mill later on in the afternoon.

The doctor's fees were beyond any working family's means but she felt sure the Faircloughs would pay once they understood the severity of Mary's condition.

'She needs a diagnosis,' Sally added, 'and, if possible, some treatment. That vapour oil he prescribed to everyone at the Hall when the fever hit last winter worked wonders. It might help Ma, too.' Fred and William exchanged a glance and there was an uncomfortable pause.

'You can ask them, Sal, but I wouldn't have thought they'll oblige,' William said eventually. A dark look had passed over his face.

'Why not?' Sally replied. 'They're usually pretty decent about things like this. Everyone who was poorly during the last bout of fever got as much medication as they needed.'

'Well, that may be so for those under their own roof,' William answered, looking at his father again. 'Let's just say that the Faircloughs don't exactly extend that level of generosity to their mill work-ers. Freda Wheeler's come down with a nasty bout of influenza and hasn't left the house for weeks.

'Bertie told us at work the other day that Julian Fairclough point blank refused to do anything for her. He wouldn't even call Dr Marshall out. Bertie's an old scoundrel all right but he loves his wife.'

'Poor Freda has enough on her mind with Bertie's drinking,' Sally answered. 'I wonder why Mr Julian refused to help. It's most unlike him.'

'We mill folk are out of sight, out of mind,' Fred said heavily as he placed a hand to his head. Sally could see the despair in his eyes.

'Well, I will certainly ask him,' she said eventually in a voice that sounded a lot stronger than she felt. 'I'll ask Mrs Hart-ley for support. Everyone knows he'll listen to her.'

Sally rushed back to the Hall in almost no time at all to find the whole of the servants' quarters buzzing in panic and disarray. Mrs Ackroyd was grim-faced as she stonily stirred a pot of soup and Mrs Hartley was pacing the floor of the servants' dining-room crying orders as she did so. Sally hadn't seen her look like this since the fever broke out last time.

'What's going on?' Sally asked Bess, who was hiding behind a mounting tower of crockery that needed washing up.

'Miss Amelia's taken ill,' she replied in a thick voice. Her eyes were looking red and her face was tearstained. 'The Faircloughs think we're about to have another bout of infection and that it might even be influenza. They've gone back to Rochdale, save Miss Amelia, of course, who's too poorly to travel. Mr Wainscot's visit is cancelled.' Bess's voice disintegrated at this point and she gave way to more sniffs and angry gasps.

Sally would have normally offered her sympathies, but it was all she could do to stop herself screaming. There was no opportunity to ask permission for Dr Marshall's assistance now. Once again the Fairclough family had retreated to their haven of safety, without any thought for their mill workers and domestic staff who were left to fight the terrors of infection without the luxury of accommodating family elsewhere.

In that moment, Sally lost all hope for her mother. It was as if her world was collapsing around her and all she could do was weep.

Unanswered Questions

The next few days passed by in a blur. Sally could barely speak to anyone around her and only shrugged mutely to Clare's persistent enquiries as to how she was feeling.

'I'm right worried about you, Sal,' she'd murmur several times a day. Sally was glad of her concern but found that the only real comfort was working herself into a state of utter oblivion where she was too tired to think.

Naturally, there was plenty of work to get stuck into at the Hall. Rachel needed a lot of care as she battled against the infection and it wasn't long before one of the stable lads fell ill, too. Miss Amelia was not an easy patient and at times it seemed that the bell from her room just wouldn't stop ringing.

'She's requested a pound of sherbet lemons,' Mrs Hartley announced one lunch time in the servants' dining-room. James, you'll head into the village later,

154

won't you, and buy her some?'

'Certainly, Mrs Hartley,' he replied quietly. Sally had been too anxious to pay much attention to James, but as she tried to force down some soup, she noticed that he looked rather pale. There was no light in his eyes as he smiled at Mrs Hartley who handed him a few pennies to pay for the sweets.

'He must be missing Nancy,' Sally remarked to Clare as they got ready for bed.

'Maybe, Sal,' Clare replied. Sally had let her friend help her with her hair again after several nights of politely declining her offers of assistance. Despite the sharp tug of the brush as Clare tackled the particularly knotty tangles, Sally was glad of the support. It wouldn't do to neglect her appearance, after all. She knew she had to maintain a brave face, for herself as much as anyone else.

'I think the rest of us are enjoying the peace,' Clare went on as she continued to brush.

The Faircloughs had taken Nancy

with them to Rochdale again as they needed her help with Miss Florence. According to Clare, she'd been none too happy about it, either.

'I don't know what she was complaining about,' Clare remarked. 'She's always on about how much she wants to get out of Brackenfold.'

'I think she means going down to London, or even abroad,' Sally answered.

'I don't think running around after Miss Florence in Rochdale is quite Nancy's idea of the great getaway!'

'No,' Clare replied as both girls giggled.

'Thanks, lovey,' Sally said, turning to squeeze her friend's hand. 'It feels right nice to think about something other than Ma for a change.'

'I'm always here for you, Sal,' Clare answered, as Sally turned back round to let her friend continue with her hair. It was much smoother now but a few stubborn tangles remained. 'I've been so worried about you ever since the Faircloughs went away.'

'I haven't been myself, I know,' Sally

replied. 'I'm just dreading going to see my family again. I'll have to tell Pa and Will that they were right all along about the Faircloughs. They've left without a care in the world for their mill staff and there's no vapour oil for Ma.' Sally could hear voice trembling as she spoke. Clare put the brush down and placed a hand on Sally's shoulder.

'You know, Sal, Adam was telling me the other day when we were out walking in the village that his brother's wife was struck by some horrible infection only a month or so ago.

'It sounds similar to what your ma has got. They asked Dr Marshall to come out to see her and they paid for the medicine themselves. They don't like to rely on the Faircloughs even though they rent their land from them.'

'Well, that's all well and good, Clare,' Sally replied as she rose from her chair. Her hair was finished now. 'But we just simply don't have the money to pay for even a minute of Dr Marshall's time, let alone any medicine.'

'The Shaws had to sell one of their best rams,' Clare answered.

'If only I had something of worth to sell,' Sally said. 'Thank you for doing my hair, by the way. It feels lovely.'

As she caught sight of her long locks in the small and slightly cracked looking-glass the girls kept by the sink in the corner of their room, Sally noticed how her curls hung softly round her face and gently brushed her shoulders as they tumbled right down to her lower back.

As she bid Clare goodnight and blew out the candle, the beginnings of an idea began to creep into the edges of her mind.

* * *

Sally continued her chores with all her usual vigour over the next few days. Both her parents had been absent from church since May Day, which wasn't like them at all. Sally had been praying with all her might for a swift recovery for Mary but found that this new idea remained in the back of her mind.

She wanted to speak with her brother before doing anything about it so would need to wait till she had some more time off work.

It was a bright and sunny Monday morning and Sally had been told to scrub the front steps. She was glad of the opportunity to work outside, even if it was hard work in the heat. It was mid-May now and the weather remained fine.

To distract herself, Sally let her thoughts drift back to Nancy's missing brooch and ribbon. There was still no news on the whereabouts of either of them and whilst Sally maintained her own private suspicions on the ribbon, the brooch was a complete mystery.

'I'd love to know where that brooch of Nancy's got to, Sal,' came a voice mirroring Sally's thoughts. James had joined her on the step with two glasses of water in his hands. 'Mrs Hartley's said to instruct you to take a break,' he explained.

Sally took the glass gratefully and the

two of them walked to one of the benches at the back of the house which the servants were permitted to use.

'Me, too,' she answered, sipping her water. It felt wonderfully cool as it hit the back of her dry and parched throat. The garden was dotted with pansies, peonies and foxgloves. The early rose bushes were bright too with gentle yellows and light pink flowers. 'It must be so frustrating for Nancy.'

'It's vexing her,' he agreed, taking a sip of his own water. Sally noticed how the skin on his hands and wrists had browned a little in the sun. She could almost feel the warmth radiating from them. His duties generally took him outside more than the maids.

'Although, I must say, Sal, she hasn't mentioned it for a while. Her mind seems,' he paused, 'elsewhere.'

'Have you . . . ' Sally started to ask, feeling that involuntary pounding in her chest once again.

'Proposed?' James finished the sentence for her. 'I have, as a matter of fact,

Sal, and, well, she said she'd have to think about it.' He sighed and Sally turned to look at him properly. She hadn't noticed before but there was a sadness and weariness in his eyes that spoke of countless sleepless nights.

'Oh, James,' she said carefully. 'You know Nancy. She'd make any fella wait, I'm sure.'

'You understand people so well, Sal,' James replied. 'I don't know how you do it.'

He was looking back at her now and for several seconds their eyes were locked in each other's gaze. Sally wasn't sure if it was her imagination, but in that moment, she felt a true connection with her long-time love.

It was as if their stories were scribbled on exactly the same scrap of paper torn from one of Mrs Hartley's ledger books, with no happy ending in sight.

'I asked her right before she was called to Rochdale,' James went on, as the moment passed. 'If I'd known I'd have held off till she returned. This is torture.'

'I understand,' Sally replied softly. She wondered if James knew how true this was.

★ ★ ★

'You want to do what, Sal? William asked incredulously when Sally stopped by the mill to see him during his break the following day on her morning off.

'It would help raise the funds for Ma,' Sally answered in what she knew was a stubborn tone.

'I don't like it, Sal,' William answered. 'What will they think at the Hall? It's not, well, normal, for young ladies, especially those in service to resort to this, you know.'

'I'm well aware of that, Will,' Sally said. 'To be honest, I hardly care any more what anyone thinks, and I've lost all hope of finding a husband, if that's what you mean.'

'I wouldn't be so sure of that, Sal,' William answered.

'And, what, exactly, would you know

about it?'

'More than you think,' William replied with a slight smile that Sally couldn't read.

'So, what do you propose we do about Ma?' she asked, feeling irritated.

'Well, Pa and I have been working extra hours,' William said. 'The extra will pay for at least a visit from Dr Marshall. Pa seems to think he has a bit saved up, too. Not much but it might pay for a bit of that vapour oil you keep going on about.'

Sally felt far from convinced as she left Will and continued on her way to pay a call on Mary. An initial consultation with the doctor was a start but she knew they'd need more money sooner or later. She didn't feel ready to abandon her idea just yet, whatever her brother might think.

Good News and Bad

May turned into June and it wasn't long before lavender was blooming in the gardens and sending its sweet, soothing scent floating down the pebbled paths and up into the warm summer air, as the temperature rose higher and higher.

Miss Amelia sat out amidst the roses in a wide straw summer hat with a floral quilted blanket draped over her lap with a cup of rosehip tea to sip as she convalesced. She'd call for Mrs Hartley to come out and read to her when her friends were otherwise engaged.

Rachel and the other infected servants recovered, too, and were back to light duties by the middle of the month. Sally returned to her parents' cottage whenever she was given time off and thankfully saw small improvements in Mary's health.

It would seem that just enough money for Dr Marshall and his medicine had been found, though Sally couldn't help but notice that the bread bin on the dresser was empty and there was nothing in the kitchen cupboard save for a few cabbages.

She bit her tongue, however, for Mary's health was clearly the most important thing for now.

Eventually the rest of the Faircloughs and their accompanying servants returned to the Hall, and for a few peaceful weeks, it felt to Sally as if life had returned to normal. Well, for the most part, that is.

Bess had remained withdrawn and sullen ever since the news came that Mr Wainscot and his valet wouldn't be calling in at Brackenfold after all.

Sally tried to include Bess as much as she could and still gave her the odd food package to take back to her mother and sister, but it was hard to do anything more. Bess even declined any more late-night lessons.

Still, in the haze of the warmest summer for years, it was almost as if the second epidemic and the missing items had never happened. Even Nancy seemed to have accepted that neither of them looked likely to turn up.

Sally realised one evening, as she was finishing off her final chores of the day, that the lady's maid hadn't mentioned the brooch or ribbon since she returned to the Hall. James was right. Her thoughts did indeed appear to be elsewhere.

It was hard to engage her in any kind of conversation. Someone would ask her to pass the sugar at the servants' dining table and she'd respond with something like 'Oh, it's another hot day, isn't it?'

'Your head's in the clouds, lass,' Mrs Ackroyd remarked grumpily several times a day, but all Nancy would do was giggle in reply. One look at the defeated expression that had now taken up permanent residence on James's face told Sally that he had yet to receive a definitive answer from Nancy.

'Oh, Sal, I have to speak with you right now,' Clare cried as she found Sally mopping the corridor floors late one afternoon. She'd just returned to the Hall from a few hours off.

Sally stopped work for a moment to speak with her friend. As she took in Clare's flushed and slightly sun-kissed face as well as the bright sparkle in her clear blue eyes, Sally had a feeling that she knew what was coming next.

'Adam's asked me to marry him!' Clare blurted out. 'We were taking our usual walk from the farm, along the valley sides where the wind is always fierce even on the sunniest day of the year, then over the beck.

'And were just looking down at Brackenfold, when he said, 'How about it, Clare. Me and you? I don't have much but I'm committed to the farm and we would even have our own little cottage on the land. Will you join me here for ever?"

'Oh, Clare, congratulations!' Sally threw her arms round her best friend as she felt her eyes fill with happy tears. 'I've known this day would come ever since we first met Adam Shaw on May Day!'

'I never guessed happiness like this existed, Sal,' Clare answered. She was crying, too. 'I'm going to be a farmer's wife!'

'Best learn how to bake pies and nurture lambs,' Sally said as she clasped Clare's hand in hers.

'I haven't the first clue, Sal,' Clare replied. 'Whatever will I do without you?'

'You won't be so far away,' Sally said brightly, trying to shield herself from the full impact of this happy news.

The girls continued to chat and eventually Clare went to fetch her own bucket to help out, as they both knew Sally would be in trouble for slacking otherwise.

Sally was glad to keep busy and Clare's excited chatter distracted her from that sinking feeling at the base of her stomach. She was to lose her best friend and there was no-one in the world who could ever replace Clare.

★ ★ ★

The next few weeks passed by. Clare was to remain in her role as housemaid for several more weeks before she'd make

168

her way to Rugged Royd for the final preparations for her wedding. She was due to leave Brackenfold right after the Rushbearing festival which took place on the village green on the last Saturday of August every year.

'I'm so glad we have Rushbearing before I'm married and off to Rugged Royd,' Clare remarked one evening as the girls got ready for bed. 'It will be one last chance to spend time with you, away from the Hall, before I become a farmer's wife.'

'Yes, I'm glad of it, too,' Sally replied, but something told her that the second summer festival of the year was likely to be bittersweet.

The servants of Brackenfold Hall looked forward to the Rushbearing festival in much the same way that May Day was greatly anticipated by all. The tradition dated back to bygone times when church floors consisted of nothing but beaten earth.

The parishioners picked rushes which grew in the fields and grassland across the valleys and placed them on top of the earth to create a pleasanter church floor. Each year, in late summer, the old rushes were cleared out of the churches and newly picked ones were taken in carts to replace them.

Over time, the rushbearing carts became more and more lavishly decorated and flamboyant in appearance, with the rushes piled up high in a haystack, transforming this rather mundane and practical task into a festival which could be enjoyed by all the community. There was music, games, food and drink stalls, plus dancing and theatre, too.

Although the floors of Brackenfold's village church, St Luke's, had long been covered in stone flags and there was no longer any need for rushes, the festival lived on. Sally liked to think that the May Day celebrations welcomed in the warmer months whilst Rushbearing waved them goodbye.

'It's strange to think that you met your Adam on May Day and were engaged by Rushbearing. Who knows where your adventures will have taken you by Christmas? There might be a baby on the way!'

'Oh, I don't know about that, Sal. These things happen in their own good time. I do wonder, though, what will come of the search for a suitor for Miss Amelia. We haven't heard anything about any potential young men for weeks and it all seems to have gone cold with Mr Wainscot, much to Bess's disappointment.'

'Yes,' Sally agreed. 'I'm sure I heard Nancy saying something to Ellie the other day about rumours that Mr Wainscot is now attached to a lady from Huddersfield. I think Miss Amelia has her heart set on going down to London for the season next year and that's why she won't make a commitment to anyone.'

'Probably,' Clare replied. 'Nancy will want to go with her, of course.'

'I know,' Sally answered, rolling her eyes. She hadn't told Clare about James's proposal to Nancy. Although she rarely kept anything from her best friend, she didn't feel this news was hers to share and didn't want to start any gossip. She knew James was hurting enough as it was and whispers amongst the other staff, no matter how good natured, would hardly do anything to help.

As she tried to drift off into sleep, it struck Sally that perhaps Nancy's reluctance to provide a straight answer for James, might have something to do with her dream of accompanying her mistress to London and potentially further afield one day. Marriage to James would most likely put a stop to that, even though Nancy would retain her place at the Hall.

There was, however, another factor that Sally couldn't quite erase from her frazzled and exhausted brain.

Try as she might, her thoughts kept returning to that enigmatic smile on her brother's face when they spoke those few weeks since, and, for some reason, Sally's mind also took her to the stunned look on Nancy's face when the only young man who'd been oblivious to her beauty on May Day night just happened to pass her his tin whistle prize.

* * *

Sally knew something bad had happened as soon as she entered the servants' dining-room the following day after completing her morning tasks. The atmosphere was heavy with tension and nobody was making eye contact with each other.

A few servants were self-consciously spooning down their porridge and drinking their tea, whilst others just stared at the floor. James was nowhere to be seen. Neither was Bess, though the odd crash and bang from the kitchen indicated she was in there somewhere. No-one spoke.

The only other sounds were the desperate sobs from Nancy as she leaned against Ellie who was awkwardly patting her back. The cries echoed round the stone walls and reverberated from the ceramic tiles on the floor.

'It's gone, I can't believe it's gone,' Sally was finally able to make out from Nancy's wails.

'What is it?' Sally mouthed at Clare who was already seated at the dining table.

'That whistle,' Clare whispered back. 'It was a gift, apparently, from May Day. It's gone missing.' Sally nodded mutely.

Something told her that now was not the time to divulge that it was her own brother who'd given the whistle to Nancy on that heady spring night several weeks ago.

'Come now, lovey,' Ellie murmured to Nancy who eventually lifted her head from Ellie's shoulder. On seeing Nancy's face, Sally gave a tiny start. The lady's maid's eyes were streaming and her face was swollen and blotchy. Nancy had been quite beautiful in her misery earlier that year but there was something almost feral about her now. Sally didn't think she'd ever seen anyone look so bereft before. It was almost as if someone had died.

The Heat Intensifies

Sally had no idea where to look or what to say. Her head was buzzing with questions but she held no hope of getting answers. Nancy's agony was piercing in its intensity. There was nothing anyone could say to console her and once again she slumped into a deep melancholia that was denser and more profound than her previous pain over the missing brooch and ribbon.

Over the next few days, Sally turned to the only coping mechanism she knew — hard graft. Yet even as she cleaned grates, beat rugs, emptied buckets, mopped floors and polished the silverware, her mind wouldn't stop buzzing with all that perplexed her.

She couldn't think who would have wanted to steal the whistle. Sally was sure it was worth less than a penny and was really nothing but a toy. The brooch had been of monetary value and the ribbon, too, albeit a fair bit less, but a tin whistle? It just didn't make any sense.

'It's almost as if someone has a personal vendetta against Nancy,' Sally remarked to Clare the next evening during their usual chat before bed.

'I know,' Clare replied. 'But who could it be? Nancy is a show off, everyone knows that, but I can't imagine anyone hating her enough to maliciously steal her things.'

'No,' Sally agreed. 'I mean, the only person here with real reason to dislike Nancy is me,' she turned to Clare to see if her friend understood her meaning. Clare gave a sympathetic nod. She was one of the very few people who knew Sally's feelings for James.

'You're not capable of thievery or malice like that, Sal. Everyone knows it.'

'I hope so,' Sally replied.

'I wonder if fingers will point towards Bess again,' Clare said quietly. 'After all, Nancy has hardly been very nice to her with all the accusations and everything.'

'Maybe,' Sally answered. She'd wondered if this might happen and had resolved to make even more of an effort with the scullery maid. Moreover, once Clare left to join Adam at Rugged Royd, Bess would be her closest female friend at the Hall.

'And goodness knows why Nancy's so bothered about that funny old whistle anyway,' Clare said with a yawn.

Sally opened her mouth to fill her in on the circumstances in which Nancy was given it, but before she could say anything, her friend started to talk about her choices for church flowers on her wedding day. This was a far pleasanter topic of conversation than speculation and gossip, so Sally held her tongue and listened to Clare chatter excitedly until both girls realised how tired they felt and finally got into their beds to sleep.

★ ★ ★

The following day, Sally made sure she poured an extra cup of tea with two sugars stirred in after the servants' evening meal to take to Bess in the kitchen, just like James used to do for her when she was scullery maid. Those days felt a lifetime ago now and part of another era.

'Cuppa for you, lovey,' she said gently, placing it on the kitchen side next to a small plate of unfinished food. Bess was looking after the steaming pots as usual.

'Thanks, Sal,' she murmured.

'You're going to eat all of that, aren't you?' Sally asked in a motherly tone. 'You work the hardest out of all of us, Bess. You need to keep your strength up.'

'Not hungry, Sal,' Bess replied. She refused to make eye contact.

'Oh, Bess, is it really that bad?' Sally asked, pulling up one of the kitchen stools to sit by her.

'I was hauled into Mr Sykes's office,' Bess said eventually. 'Mrs Ackroyd was there, too, and Mrs Hartley. They were asking me all sorts of questions. You know, about how I came by that yellow ribbon and if I had anything against Nancy.'

'Gosh,' Sally answered, 'what did you say?'

'Told them the truth — that I don't

know owt,' Bess replied with a shrug. 'Mrs Ackroyd was watching me with those beady little eyes of hers and kept shaking her head.' Bess lowered her voice.

Nancy hadn't come down for any meals since the tin whistle went missing and the cook was still in the servants' dining-room next door polishing off a generous portion of cottage pie.

Sally could hear her loud voice booming out over all the others. Still, she knew Bess needed to be careful. You never knew who could be listening and the walls were thin, after all.

'I'm glad Mrs Hartley was there,' Sally said in the same hushed tone. 'She won't let them accuse you of anything without any proof.'

'Yes, Sal. You were right about her,' Bess replied, her voice lightening a little. She even looked Sally directly in the eye for a short while. 'She kept telling me not to worry and even told Mrs Ackroyd to go easy on me at one point. She's actually really nice.'

'I knew you'd see that one day,' Sally smiled. 'Now, you know that our Clare is about to be married to Adam Shaw and will be leaving us soon.' The words stuck a little in her throat but she kept her voice bright and her face composed for Bess's sake. 'So we'll need a new housemaid. What do you think?'

'Won't Ellie want the job?' Bess answered flatly as she returned to stirring the pots.

'Well, you've got as good a chance as her, and if she does get it, I'm sure you'll move up the ranks to kitchen maid in her place. It does get easier here, Bess, after you've done your time at the bottom.'

Bess simply shrugged and muttered something Sally couldn't quite make out. She thought she heard something about 'nothing really mattering any more', but before she had time to ask what Bess meant the other servants were scraping their chairs on the floor as they left the room for the last stage of the day's work.

She'd be in for some grief from Mrs Ackroyd if she didn't make a move.

'See you soon, lovey,' she said to Bess as she left the kitchen.

The weeks rolled by and it wasn't long before the Rushbearing festival was only a few days away. The sun continued to rule the skies and it felt as if the world was roasting in its blaze.

The folk of Brackenfold had gone from praising the wonderful weather to praying for the temperature to drop. The ground was parched, the summer flowers were wilting and the grasslands looked more like hayfields. Sally longed for a downpour of rain to clear the air and hydrate the earth. Surely it had to come soon.

'Hot enough for you, Sal?' Fred laughed by way of greeting when Sally called by her parents' cottage. It was the first Saturday afternoon she'd had off for a few weeks now.

'I'd say so.' She laughed, taking a gulp of water from the glass bottle that she'd brought from the Hall. She'd had to stop by the water pump near her parents' house to refill it. It had felt fiery underfoot as she'd walked, as if smouldering coals were burning just below the surface of the roads.

Sally could feel sweat building up under her straw hat and was pleased to remove it once she was indoors. The air was stagnant and stuffy inside, however, and the relief was short-lived.

'I've right had enough of it now, Sal,' Mary agreed from the armchair. She'd made herself a fan from one of the ledger sheets from the mill and was wafting the air backwards and forwards with it.

'How are you feeling now, Ma, in terms of your health, I mean?'

'Oh apart from being a human furnace, I'm not too bad now, lovey,' Mary answered. 'I'm back at the looms, so I'm tired, of course, but I can't complain and I feel very lucky.'

'So do I,' Sally said as she leaned over to squeeze her mother's hand. 'I can't tell you how worried I've been, Ma.'

'Well, it's behind us now, Sal,' Mary answered. 'So no more of that. Tell me the news from the Hall. I heard that Nancy's had a pipe or something pinched now.'

'A tin whistle.' Sally giggled.

It was funny how stories changed as they passed down the Brackenfold gossip trail. Fred had closed his eyes for a Saturday afternoon snooze. He'd never been very interested in the village grapevine.

'Someone said it was a gift from her new sweetheart or something,' Mary went on, raising her eyebrows at Sally. 'Isn't she attached to James any longer?'

'Goodness knows what's going on, Ma,' Sally answered. There was a feeling she couldn't identify flickering right in her chest and suddenly she felt more alert and alive than she had done for months. She wanted to tell Mary about what she'd seen on May Day night, but something told her to tread carefully for now.

'Where's William today?' she asked.

'Oh, I don't know, Sal. We don't see so much of him these days, apart from at work, of course. He has carried on with some extra hours in the mill, I know that much, but otherwise I haven't a clue.'

'Tell him I was asking after him, won't you,' Sally said.

She reminded her mother to pass the message on to her brother when she said goodbye, a short while later. That flickering feeling from before stayed with Sally all the way back to the Hall, like a tiny candle glowing in her heart.

The Truth Dawns

The air still felt hot as Sally retraced her steps, even though the sun was making its way towards the west now. The sky was a flawless and brilliant shade of blue. Sally could hear birds calling to each other and the gentle hum of insects in the grass.

It wasn't long before she'd passed the great gates and was walking along the tree-lined terrace to the house. As the Hall came into view, Sally couldn't help marvelling for a moment at the place she called home.

Sunbeams glinted from the tall windows and the many red chimney pots were stark against the blue of the sky. Leafy ivy crept up the brickwork.

For a second Sally let herself imagine that she was Miss Amelia herself out for a late afternoon stroll and was arriving back home for a refreshing iced lemonade served in a crystal glass with an assortment of fancy cakes and sweetmeats.

She slowed her pace to put off her return to the servants' door for as long as possible. She could almost hear Mrs Ackroyd's scornful laughter in her ear but chose to ignore it. Her imaginary world was no-one's realm but hers.

'All right, Sal.' James's soft voice gave Sally a little start as it cut into her dreamy daze. He'd come up from behind and had clearly picked up his pace to reach her. She hadn't expected to come across any of the other servants on her trip back to the Hall.

'Is it your afternoon off, too, James?' she asked.

'Aye,' he replied. 'I've just been to see Pa for a few hours.' James's father lived in Brackenfold. 'It's a right nice evening, Sal. Come and have a quick walk with me round the grounds. Mrs Hartley won't mind us having another fifteen minutes or so, I'm sure.'

'I don't know, James. We're supposed to be back for half past five and it's twenty past now.'

'Come on, Sal. Just a quick one.' James

brushed Sally's arm gently with the back of his hand as she eventually smiled and nodded.

The sun had crept even further to the west now and its intensity was over for another day. A welcome breeze was ruffling the tendrils of hair that were escaping from her straw hat. The apple tree in one corner of the Brackenfold gardens was covered in apples and a few had even fallen to the ground.

'How are things with you, Sal?' James asked after the two of them had walked for several minutes in a companionable silence.

'Not so bad, thanks, James,' Sally responded. 'I'll miss Clare once she goes to the farm, but my ma seems to be on the mend, so that's good news.'

'I'm glad, Sal. I know how much you love your ma,' James replied quietly. He'd lost his own mother a few years ago to influenza.

'How are you, James?' Sally asked.

'Oh, you know. Same old for me.' Sally wondered if he'd mention Nancy and wasn't sure if it would be polite to ask if she'd given him an answer yet. 'Still no word from Nance,' James went on, as if reading her thoughts.

'That must be hard,' Sally murmured. A delicate peacock butterfly flew in front of them in a flutter of amber, sapphire and red. It eventually settled on some of the sweet scented lavender that was growing near the pebbled path.

'It is, Sal. Well, it was,' James responded slowly. 'At first the wait was unbearable but as time's gone on without any answer, it's not so intense, if you know what I mean. It's also given me time to think.'

'Do you still want to marry Nancy, James?' Sally hoped he couldn't hear the anticipation in her voice.

'I honestly don't know, Sal,' he answered, shaking his head. 'Somehow, I don't feel I know Nancy these days. I know she's upset about her things going missing and all that, but the way she spoke to Bess made me pretty uncomfortable. You can't go around hurling accusations like that.'

'I felt the same,' Sally answered, unable to keep her opinions to herself. 'Bess has a hard time here and has problems back home. She might not be the friendliest lass at the Hall, but she's no thief, I'm sure of it.'

'I bought Nance a new yellow ribbon, you know, after her first one went missing,' James went on. 'But I don't think I've ever seen her wear it. She even left it on the dining-room table downstairs when I first gave it to her. I had to run after her with it before she remembered.'

'Goodness,' Sally murmured as they made their way back to the Hall. She wanted to say how ungrateful and rude she found this behaviour, but felt she'd given James enough of her thoughts for now. In any case, it was time to resume their duties.

'I wouldn't put someone I loved through misery like this, that's for sure,' James added.

'Nor would I,' Sally answered softly. The peacock butterfly was back, though this time, a small tortoiseshell butterfly had joined it too. They flew closely together like airborne flowers dancing in the light summer breeze. At times it was almost impossible to tell them apart.

When Sally bid James goodbye at the servants' front door, she found that the flickering she'd felt in her chest earlier that day had returned and was showing no sign of going away.

As she made her way back to her room, to change into her uniform for her evening duties, Sally finally managed to identify that feeling — it was hope.

Rushbearing Time

The familiar sunbeams woke Sally up bright and early on the morning of the Rushbearing festival.

'Another holiday, Sal! How exciting.'

Clare was already out of bed and dressed in a flowing marigold dress with a green sash round the middle. Unlike May Day, there were no customs around clothing for Rushbearing, though the folk of Brackenfold liked to look their best.

'I might spend this one up here,' Sally groaned turning over. Every limb in her body was aching. She must have beaten eight ornate rugs the night before. 'As much as I love Rushbearing, I love my bed more!'

'Nonsense, Sal, it's our last day out together before I become a married woman!'

'Only joking,' Sally answered as she heaved herself up from the sheets. 'You know I wouldn't miss this for the world.'

She'd already chosen her nicest sky blue dress with a white lace sash for the occasion.

As Clare helped her put up her hair, Sally felt a tiny knot of anticipation form in her stomach and nervous excitement fluttered in her chest. She found herself wondering whether James might look at her differently in these clothes. She hadn't worn this frock since Rushbearing last year.

'I'm not sure Bess will be as good as you with my hair,' Sally remarked.

She'd noticed Clare's small trunk in the corner of the bedroom and felt that familiar pang of sadness strike through her heart. One of Adam's brothers was due to pick it up later with his horse and cart and take it over to Rugged Royd Farm.

Clare would spend the next week or so sharing a room with one of Adam's sisters before they finally tied the knot and moved into their own cottage together.

'She may have hidden talents.' Clare giggled though Sally could tell that she was feeling a little upset.

'No more of that,' Sally whispered. 'Today is a happy day and I really am thrilled you've found Adam.'

'We'll always be best friends, Sal,' Clare replied. 'I can promise you that.'

It wasn't long before the two house-maids had eaten a swift breakfast and were off with the other servants to the village green to start the Rushbearing festivities.

Sally had hoped they might walk with James but he was further to the front of the group. She was reassured, however, that Nancy was nowhere to be seen. Ellie said she'd left the Hall earlier and made her way to the green on her own. The sun beat down as they walked and it wasn't long before Sally was gulping down the water she'd bought with her in her glass bottle.

'Thunder's coming,' an old man said as they passed.

'There's hardly a cloud in the sky!' Clare said, shaking her head.

'The air's changed,' he answered

before tipping his hat and making his way off in the opposite direction.

'It does feel different today, actually,' Sally remarked as they continued to walk. 'The air feels closer somehow and quite sticky.'

'I think he's talking nonsense,' Clare replied with a shrug. 'Oh, I can hear the music, Sal! We're nearly there.'

A few moments later, they'd turned a corner and were on the village green, which was decked out once again in lots of festive finery. Villagers had hung bunting and lanterns outside their houses in much the same way as they'd done for May Day.

The same band had situated themselves in the centre of the green, too, though of course there was no maypole this time. A group of mummers in fancy dress and masks had congregated where the maypole had stood in preparation for a show later on. Sally spotted two knights, a jester and a doctor.

The story was the same every year. There would be a mock duel whilst the jester bounced around entertaining the crowd and the band played. When one knight finally fell, the doctor would arrive with a magical medicine to revive him. Some of the servants complained that the mummers' play was boring, but Sally rather liked the familiarity of it all. It reminded her of being a child.

The Morris dancers had formed a small group, too, as had the men who would pull the rushbearing cart, which would arrive any time now. They were dressed in white and wore wide-brimmed dark hats and clogs.

The sugary smells of candyfloss, hot chocolate and other sweet treats were drifting on the gentle breeze. Like May Day, the green was full of vendors selling refreshments, sweets and hot food.

Sally looked around for her parents who usually joined in with the festivities. Folk from neighbouring villages had turned up, too, so there was quite a crowd of people by now, and plenty of faces Sally didn't recognise. She was glad to see, however, that Bess was standing nearby, arm in arm with her sister, Meg. They were both neatly turned out in old but clean and respectable clothes. Meg had a little more colour in her cheeks, too. Their mother must have let them out for once. Sally hoped this was a sign that things were improving at home.

'Are you going to look for Adam?' she asked Clare.

'Later, Sal,' Clare replied. 'I've already told him that I want to spend most of today with you. We have the rest of our lives to spend together, after all.'

The two girls linked arms and went to buy some cooling lemonade. Sally resolved to look for her family later and would even try to forget about James for a little while. It was time to savour every last possible moment with her best friend.

Once they'd purchased their drinks, the girls sat down on a spare patch grass to enjoy the sweet and citrusy tang of the lemonade.

'Look, Sal, the cart's arrived!' Clare

squealed after a few minutes had passed. Her eyes were fixed on the horse-drawn wagon that had just appeared round the bend in the lane. The men in the wide-brimmed hats hurried over and began pulling the cart towards the green as the horses were led away. As usual, it was piled high in a tall haystack of green rushes. There were cries and cheers as the crowd welcomed the cart.

Paid for by the Faircloughs, the front of the cart bore their family crest of the golden eagle and white stag, but this year the wagon had been painted in a fresh coat of crimson red and dotted with delicate white flowers.

There were yet more cheers as one of the Faircloughs' carriages pulled up, too, and Miss Amelia made her grand entrance. Dressed in a gown of the same crimson as the cart, she also wore an elaborate white hat with a great many feathers and a large bejewelled pin which shone and glinted in the sunlight.

Sally had heard somewhere that at other Rushbearing festivals, the village girls took it in turns to ride on the cart as it made its way to the church, but, rather like the position of May Queen, Miss Amelia had claimed this role for herself and had been the sole occupant of the rushbearing cart since childhood.

Just as she was smiling and waving to the crowd, there came a flurry of extra squeals and coos, for Miss Florence had also alighted from the carriage and was wearing a miniature replica of Miss Amelia's dress. She was uncharacteristically subdued today and her solemn round face was framed by beautiful blonde curls which hung from her white hat. Quickly, Rachel ushered her over to the wagon and lifted her up on to it. It would seem Miss Amelia had finally agreed to share her special perch with her young niece this year.

Miss Amelia continued to wave and blow kisses to the crowd once the pair were settled on the cart, whilst Miss Florence remained quiet as she took everything in.

Sally wondered if this new experience

was somewhat unnerving for the small child and thought perhaps it might take some time for her to decide whether or not she liked it.

No-one noticed that the breeze had turned into more of a wind until a gust sent a few hats flying off in the air. Sally and Clare smiled and waved as they enjoyed the relief from the heat as the cart picked up speed. It wasn't far to St Luke's, the village church, so, rather like the May Day procession, the cart would go the scenic route round the houses of Brackenfold first.

From nowhere Sally felt a slight shiver and looked up to see that the sun was hiding behind a mass of dark clouds that had appeared as if by magic and were now covering most of the sky.

'Where on earth have they come from?' Clare muttered next to her.

'I think that old fella might have been right after all,' Sally replied. 'It would seem thunder is on the way.'

'Sal,' came a familiar voice, and the girls looked up to see William elbowing his way through the villagers. Sally took one look at his face and felt sick. Something was dangerously wrong.

The Sky Darkens

William's face was ashen and his eyes were dark. He hadn't dressed up for the occasion and was wearing an old pair of trousers without any braces and a crumpled shirt with no necktie either.

'What is it, Will?' Sally asked. She could hear the anxiety in her hoarse and breathless voice.

'It's Ma,' he replied grimly. 'She took a sudden turn for the worse last night or maybe it's a new infection, I don't know. Her temperature's sky high but she can't stop shivering and won't leave her bed. She's coughing every five minutes and I can hear her chest wheeze with the effort. She's in so much pain, Sal. It's right horrible to see.'

'I must go to her,' Sally said, taking a step forwards as she did so.

'No, Sal. She can barely speak and Pa's there now.'

'Nonsense. I should be there, Will. I can look after them both.'

'Actually, Sal, Nancy's with them now and is doing a grand job.' William's eyes were darting around nervously and he had the grace to look embarrassed.

'Nancy?' Sally whispered in disbelief as she rounded on her brother with her hands on her hips. Her shock turned into outrage and her voice gained momentum. 'You need to explain yourself to me, William Halfpenny. Right now.'

'I know, Sal, and I will, I promise. But right now, we need to focus on Ma.'

'I don't care if the queen herself is at our cottage,' Sally answered, feeling her face harden and her voice get louder still. 'My mother is ill and she needs me. I'm her daughter.'

'Actually, Sal, I think what she needs is more medicine and another visit from Dr Marshall. I really didn't want it to come to this, and you know I don't approve, but if you're still willing, Sal, you know, to do what you suggested before, I think it would be a good idea. I hate to ask, but I don't know what else to do.' Sally could hear the desperation in his voice.

She looked out over the village green. The merriment continued, of course, as if nothing had happened. She wanted to scream at everybody to stop. Her ma was in trouble and today was no longer a time for celebration.

A whoop broke out amongst the crowd as Miss Amelia and Miss Florence commenced their ride on the rushbearing cart. Sally spotted Mr Julian and the older Mr Fairclough standing at the front of the crowd as they clapped and cheered with everybody else. Frustrated tears formed in Sally's eyes. They truly had no idea of the hardships faced by the likes of her family. No idea at all.

'Sal,' Clare's voice came from beside her. Sally had almost forgotten she was there. 'Let me talk to Adam. They might have some medicine left from when his sister-inlaw was poorly. It's worth a shot.'

'Thank you, Clare, but no. I know how to help my ma and it's something I need to do on my own. The answer's yes, Will, and I will see to it right now.' Sally found to her surprise that the early panic had been replaced by an almost eerie sense of calm.

She was focused now entirely on the task in hand and knew she could waste no more time. She embraced Clare, told her to go and find Adam and murmured her apologies that their special day together had to be curtailed. She hugged William and told him to wait for her back at the cottage. She'd be as quick as she could.

Sally felt a cool breeze nip the back of her neck as she weaved her way through the crowd. She could hear ladies complaining about the drop in temperature around her.

No-one had thought to bring a cloak or shawl. It was the first time in weeks that anyone in Brackenfold had felt remotely chilly at all. Overhead the clouds remained dark and angry.

None of this mattered to Sally, of course. The discourse around her was devoid of any meaning and the village merry-makers were nothing but an inconvenient barrier she must pass on her mission to help Ma.

'Sal!'

She was vaguely aware that someone had been calling her name for a while now, but the world around her remained part of another dimension in which she had no place. It might as well have been another play performed by the mummers as far as Sally was concerned. She ignored the voice and ploughed on.

Having almost reached the edge of the village green, there wasn't far to go now. Still, she had no choice but to be drawn out of her trance and come to a halt when James eventually caught up with her.

'By heck, Sal. What's got into you?' His face was flushed from running. 'I've chased you all the way up the green. What's wrong?'

'My ma's poorly again, James,' Sally said, as tried to keep her voice even. The wash of calm she'd felt before had gone and she was back to feeling panicky again. 'I have to help her and I know how I can, but I need to go and get on with it.' She picked up her pace but James kept up with her.

'How, Sal? Tell me.'

'I haven't time right now. And I don't want you to talk me out of it,' Sally replied.

'Come on, Sal. At least give me a bit more than that. I might be able to help.'

'I need some money to pay for Dr Marshall's vapour oil,' Sally answered relenting a little. 'It may be our last chance. I know how I can raise some and I'm going to get started on it now.'

'Ask the master,' James replied. 'I would have thought he'd pay for it.'

'I don't think he will,' Sally replied shortly. 'He wouldn't help Freda Wheeler when she came down with influenza recently and I'm worried he'll be the same about Ma. I can't wait around for him to decide, either. She needs help now.'

She saw James's face change. It went as dark as the clouds up above.

'Don't do anything rash, Sal. I've heard the odd bit of gossip from round the village. People round here like to talk, you know.'

'What do you mean?' Sally cried, feeling alarmed. A swirl of anger and confusion had started to rise from deep within her stomach. Just then, however, the crowd surged upon them. Neither Sally nor James had noticed but the rush-bearing cart holding Miss Amelia and Miss Florence was now heading right in their direction, along with the band who were following them. Hastily Sally and James got out of its way. It was all they could do to avoid being trampled on by the over-enthusiastic festival-goers, too.

Sally turned to James to wait for his reply, but in that moment her eye was caught by something that was going on in the cart. Miss Florence, who was sitting on Miss Amelia's lap appeared to be reaching for something in her hair. They were whisked past too quickly for Sally to see anything more and anyway, she knew she had to continue her conversation with James even though it was almost impossible to hear him, thanks to the whoops, cheers, bangs of the drum and toots of the horns.

Amidst the tangled mish-mash of words, Sally heard James shout something about folk knowing now who'd been stealing and that the village streets were full of whispered accusations which were making their way to the Hall.

'You can't think that I have anything to do with any of this,' she yelled through the noise of the crowd. James could only give her an uncomfortable shrug by way of reply. 'I don't much care for Nancy but I'd never resort to stealing and selling her things. I thought you knew me better than that, James! I thought we were friends.'

As more angry tears tumbled down her cheeks, Sally turned and fled. As she ran back to Brackenfold Hall the first drops of rain began to fall from the thunderous sky overhead.

The Real Thief

As Sally ran down the streets, she paid no attention to the cool splashes of rain as they soaked her hat, her hair and her dress. They mingled with the hot tears which still ran down her face. The world was a blurry wet muddle of pain and confusion.

At one point she thought she could hear a voice crying out her name but she wouldn't stop this time. She'd had enough of James Armstrong and wouldn't waste any more of her time on him. She only wished she'd learned of his true nature before now and hadn't spent so many nights crying over him. He wasn't worth her tears. She knew that now. She needed to focus on Ma.

Sally finally stopped running when she reached the Hall grounds. She was out of breath and uncomfortably hot, despite the heavy rain. Thunder had begun to grumble and roar too. It wouldn't be too long now till lightning would flash above the valley towns.

Sally had a feeling the Rushbearing festivities might come to an early finish and she needed to focus on the job in hand before the other servants returned. She walked through the grounds and towards the servants' entrance, waving away the inquisitive greeting from the gardener who was sheltering in the stables, having been left to keep an eye on the Hall whilst everyone else was at the festival.

Sally's first port of call should have been the kitchen and then her bedroom to change out of her sodden best clothes and get to work, but for some reason she found herself heading instead for Miss Florence's nursery.

Sally's brain was in overdrive and she knew she didn't have much time, but something told her that she was closer now than ever to solving the mystery of Nancy's missing treasures.

She thought back to the way Miss Florence had been reaching up to Miss Amelia's hair. There had been a steely determination in the child's eyes. Sally was fairly sure that she knew what the little girl was after; it was that beautiful shiny hairpin that had gleamed so delightfully in the sunlight, before the storm clouds took over.

Sally opened the nursery door. She didn't know the room very well as Rachel did most of the dusting alongside her nursing duties but from time to time she'd been called in to give it a good once over. But Sally had no intention of doing any cleaning today. Instead, she opened the bottom drawers to see what they contained, but all she could see were the frills of Miss Florence's tiny dresses. Next she looked under her pillow and then, finding nothing, she tried searching amidst the little girl's large collection of china dolls which sat on a low shelf in one corner of the room.

They stared at her with their beady glass eyes until she felt rather unnerved and had to look away. There was nothing to be found there anyway. The small army of wooden toy soldiers at the

211

bottom of the wardrobe held no bounty either.

The rain was still lashing against the walls and windows of the Hall and outside she could see big forks of lightning across the valley. She thought she could hear voices and shrieks outside. Nerves and panic fluttered in her chest. She knew she didn't have long left.

Sally looked around the room, hoping for inspiration from somewhere. The walls were covered with colourful paintings of circus tents, clowns, acrobats and exotic-looking animals from faraway lands.

Sally had only ever had one rag doll when she grew up. The very idea of a room of her own was the stuff of make-believe. When she thought back to the little bed her mother would make up for her in front of the kitchen range, however, Sally felt a stab of nostalgia and more than a little compassion for the wilful Miss Florence. Despite her roomful of lovely things, life must be rather lonely for her, with only her nursemaid for company most of the time.

Sally was just beginning to wonder whether she had in fact been wrong all along, when she caught sight of the doll's house on the other side of the room. Standing at two feet high, it was an impressive structure and Sally found it hard to believe that such time, skill and workmanship had been devoted to an imaginary home. To call it a toy seemed something of an insult.

The façade of the house was elegantly carved and painted sky blue. It had pretty bay windows and delicately painted rose and ivy plants crept up the sides. Sally tried to peer through the windows, without having to touch the house, but it was impossible to see properly. She wasn't giving up just yet.

On closer examination, the façade of the house was actually two panels on hinges which could be gently pulled apart to reveal the rooms inside. As she did so, Sally realised her hands were trembling. Causing a breakage simply didn't bear thinking about. Sally said a silent prayer of thanks when the panels separated without incident and she was able to peruse the inside of the house.

Sally couldn't help but marvel for a moment at the stunning interior. It was the perfect home in miniature, complete with a drawing-room, ballroom, fully equipped kitchen, dining-room, parlour and servants' quarters. The rooms were populated with tiny figures waiting patiently for Miss Florence to return and bring them to life.

Sally's inner child danced with joy as she fought the urge to surrender to her imagination and explore some more.

Reluctantly she kept to the task in hand and it wasn't long before her eye was drawn to something shiny and her heart leaped with the revelation that she had, in fact, been correct all the time. For stuffed under the four-poster bed in the master bedroom was the beautiful ornate brooch that Nancy had lost last spring.

Swiftly, Sally pulled it out and placed it in the pocket of her dress. Now for the tin whistle which was too big surely to be hidden within the house. She peeped behind it instead, and wasn't surprised to see the toy tucked neatly at the back. She popped it in her pocket too and then made her way back to the kitchen to borrow a pair of Mrs Ackroyd's scissors. She still had plenty of work to do.

The rain had finally stopped when Sally returned to the servants' dining-room a couple of hours later. The other servants were sitting round the table with mugs of hot tea. Bess was handing out plates of bread and dripping.

Clare must have returned to Rugged Royd Farm with the Shaws for she was nowhere to be seen. Sally realised with a pang how much she missed her best friend already.

Some, like Sally, had changed into dry clothes, but she noticed that James remained in his damp shirt and breeches. He looked particularly wretched and forlorn.

Nancy had returned to the Hall too and sat at a little distance from everyone else. She was wrapped up in a large grey cloak.

'Good evening,' Sally said to the room. Her voice sounded louder and much more confident than she felt inside. 'If the senior team are agreeable, I would like to address the staff.' Mr Sykes shuffled uncomfortably in his seat, Mrs Ackroyd raised her eyebrows but Mrs Hartley gave Sally a tiny nod and half-smile which was all the permission she needed.

'We all owe Bess an apology,' she started. The scullery maid had finished handing out the bread and dripping now and was standing by the door to the kitchen. 'I saw Miss Florence trying to grab Miss Amelia's hairpin on the rush-bearing cart earlier today,' Sally went on. 'And it struck me that the little girl might be drawn to shiny and sparkly things. I followed my hunch and had a look in the nursery just now and found these things hidden away in her doll's-house.' There was a collective gasp as Sally placed the brooch and whistle on the table.

'Miss Florence is a bit of a magpie,' Rachel said after a while. 'Only the other day I had to stop her from clambering up one of the banisters. She was trying to reach the chandelier.' Sally stole a peep at Nancy. She had her hands over her face and was trembling a little.

'She must have seen me with them when I was looking after her,' Nancy said from behind her palms. 'And then managed to take them at some point without me noticing.'

'What a little madam,' Rachel said incredulously. 'I should have noticed.'

'So should I,' Nancy murmured. She still hadn't looked up to face the others.

'What about that yellow ribbon, then?' Mrs Ackroyd asked eventually, though her voice held none of its usual authority.

'I can answer that,' Bess was standing by the kitchen door but moved closer to the others as she spoke. 'That Mr Crookshanks fella did give it to me,' she said. 'He said he saw it and thought of me, so I figured he'd bought it in a shop. I didn't want to say owt to anyone as you'd all have started gossiping. I thought he'd be coming back to see me again. He promised he would.' Bess's eyes had filled with tears now and her voice wavered a little.

Instinctively, Sally walked over to her and placed her hand on her arm.

'I didn't believe it at first, but I think now that it probably is Nancy's ribbon and he either pinched it or found it lying on the floor,' Bess went on as the tears started to fall.

'I wrote him so many letters, after you taught me how to, Sal, and he never once replied.' She took the piece of yellow ribbon from her apron pocket. 'Here, Nancy. You might as well have it back.'

'Swap,' Nancy replied. She took the ribbon and then picked up the ornate brooch from the table and placed it in Bess's hands. She'd taken the tin whistle from the table, too, but kept tight hold of that.

'I can't, Nancy.' Bess looked shocked and quite overcome.

'It's only right,' Nancy replied, sounding choked. 'I'm sorry, Bess. Truly I am.' Her tears were falling freely now and, although she looked like she had some more to say, her words were swallowed by sobs.

'It's all right,' Bess muttered awkwardly as she examined the brooch. Her eyes were still wet with tears.

Sally cleared her throat.

'There comes a time, Bess,' she started, 'when we have to accept that there's nothing more we can do to win over a person whose heart is clearly elsewhere and realise that we deserve someone who can reciprocate our love.' She looked everywhere but James.

'Now, if you'll excuse me, my ma needs my attention. As some of you already know, she's taken a turn for the worse and I need some money for Dr Marshall's services and his vapour oil. So, I've decided to sell the only asset I have; my hair.' There was a gasp around the room as Sally removed her cap to reveal the cropped short bob underneath.

'Your beautiful curly locks, Sal,' Ellie

murmured in disbelief, but Sally was unrepentant.

'Love takes us in strange directions sometimes,' she went on. 'And that's partly why I've made another big decision. I'm leaving Brackenfold Hall. I'm moving back to my parents to take care of my ma and when she's better I'll present myself to Fairclough's Mill. I've already stated my intention to Mr Julian in writing and will ask my father to call by later for my things. Now, I really must be going. Good night.'

And with that, Sally quickly embraced Bess, Rachel, Ellie and Mrs Hartley before raising her hand to the rest of the staff.

For the third time that day, she thought she could hear someone calling her name as she ran out of the servants' door and down the path, but, once again, she didn't look back.

Two Weeks Later

Sally stood in front of the loom and tried not to panic. It was only her second day in the mill but her head was already spinning. She didn't think she'd ever been given so much information before.

She'd been placed in the weaving shed under the command of senior weaver, Matilda White, who was a large and fierce woman who'd already given Sally a dressing down for getting her lines of yarn all muddled up.

It was hard not to be intimidated by the huge and noisy steam-powered looms. The weaving shed was uncomfortably hot, too, and Sally worried there wasn't enough light to see properly.

She observed the others from the corner of her eye. Sally would have given anything to be able to work with their speed and confidence and could barely believe that any of them had ever been new to the mill.

She found herself longing for a grate

to clean, some silver to polish and even a dirty floor to scrub.

Her entire being buzzed with anxiety, confusion and more than a little regret.

'It'll be strange at first, Sal, but you'll get used to it,' William had told her as she'd struggled to eat her breakfast the previous day. He'd been delighted when she told him of her plans. 'I've been telling you for ages to leave that place,' he'd said.

The days following her departure from the Hall had felt like a scary and unnatural dream. It hadn't taken William long to find a buyer for Sally's hair and the money had helped pay for another consultation with Dr Marshall and a week's worth of vapour oil as well.

Sally had refused to leave Mary and even slept by her side. Not that rest came easily, however. As the days went by, oblivion seemed further and further away.

Fred had insisted that he take Sally to Clare's wedding, and though she enjoyed seeing her best friend exchange vows with Adam, Sally had barely been able to concentrate.

'Go back to your ma,' Clare had whispered when Sally came to congratulate her afterwards. 'She needs you more than I do.'

'You promised to tell me what's going on between you and Nancy,' Sally had said to William after she returned home from the church. Mary had fallen into a deep sleep.

'Oh, yes, Sal, we're courting,' he replied as he handed her a cup of tea. 'I'd have thought you would have guessed that by now.'

'Why didn't you tell me sooner?' Sally asked.

'Well, to be honest, we haven't been attached for very long,' he answered. 'After May Day, she kept turning up at the mill on her days off with baskets of sandwiches and such like. I didn't have much of a clue of what was going on till one of my mates mentioned that she was sweet on me and was no longer attached to James.' Sally laughed in spite of herself and shook her head.

'You men are impossible,' she said.

* * *

After a week of bed rest and vapour oil, the Halfpennys' prayers were answered and Mary began to improve.

'I don't care what you say, it's time you retired from the mill,' Sally told her, once she was well enough to sit in the myrtle green armchair downstairs.

'I think I'll take your advice, for once,' Mary answered with a half-smile. The fever had taken its toll on her. She looked frailer than ever. 'But what's all this about you joining the mill, Sal? I've told you before that the Hall offers much better work. Do you really feel that you can't return?'

'Oh, yes,' Sally answered, though she couldn't stop the tears welling up in her eyes. 'Clare's gone now, hasn't she, and there's nothing and no-one there for me any more.'

Try as she might she couldn't get the look on James's face at Rushbearing out of her head.

Surprising News

Realising she'd been lost in her thoughts, Sally returned to the loom. She just couldn't shake off the fear that she was about to ruin some yarn or, worse still, lose a finger. There was no sign of her brother or father anywhere. Bravery was her only choice now.

'Sally Halfpenny,' a voice boomed. Sally looked up, expecting to see the formidable Matilda White bearing over her, but the senior weaver was standing by the shed door with one hand on her hip and a disapproving look on her face. The person striding towards her, looking rather uncomfortable but determined nevertheless, was Mrs Ackroyd.

She looked so different in her outdoor coat and bonnet that Sally had to look twice to check it was definitely the cook from the Hall.

'Mrs Ackroyd, what on earth are you doing here?' Sally asked, but then let out a tiny scream, for behind her, came Mrs

Hartley, Bess, Rachel, Ellie, Nancy and James. From nowhere Fred and William appeared and it wasn't long before they'd all formed a huddle around Sally.

'We've come with Mr Julian and his wife's blessing,' Mrs Hartley explained, stepping forward. 'And we've left Mr Sykes holding the fort.

'Miss Florence has been entrusted to her mother's care for once and we've asked them to give her a stern talking to about taking other people's things.

'Anyway, we're here because we all feel very strongly that we'd like you to return to the Hall, Sally. The place, quite simply, isn't the same without you.'

'Oh, that's very kind of you, but I've accepted a new job here now,' Sally answered quietly.

'I can help with that,' Bess replied. Sally noticed that there was a brightness to her eyes again and the confidence she'd found before appeared to have returned.

'Our Meg's got a job in the mill now,' Bess went on. 'I'd like to work alongside her and move home. Our aunt's retired from work and moved from Dewsbury to live with us. She can keep Ma company, so Meg can get a job here. It means the master can sort us out with a decent cottage.

'I never really took to life in the Hall, Sal. It didn't suit me, but I think I might be better with the looms. Mr Julian said I can have your job here.'

'You wouldn't return to the role of scullery maid,' Mrs Hartley cut in quickly. 'We haven't appointed a new housemaid and your old job is waiting for you. Ellie is Clare's replacement.'

'But you never know what might happen soon, Sally,' Nancy said quietly.

'It's been confirmed that Miss Amelia is going to London in March next year for the social season. I think it's a last-ditch attempt to find her a husband. Of course, she'll need her maid with her so I'll be going, too.'

Nancy stole a look at William.

'Your brother will also be making his way down south, actually, and will look for employment there. We plan to find out what life has in store for us in London.

'The Faircloughs don't need to know about our engagement just yet. As soon as William's found work, I'll hand in my notice to Miss Amelia and we'll be wed.'

'Really, Will?' Sally shot a shocked look at her brother who smiled sheepishly. Fred looked both proud and exasperated at the same time.

'I was waiting for the right time to tell you,' William answered quietly. 'Please don't tell Ma just yet.'

'So there might be a lady's maid job going soon,' Mrs Hartley added. 'And we can't think of anyone better for the job than you.'

Sally heard the emotion building in the older woman's voice.

'We miss you, Sally,' Mrs Hartley said. 'Your kindness is a rare thing indeed. And we'd all like you back. Me especially.'

'Well, when you put it like that, what else can I say?' Sally said eventually. She knew her voice sounded choked.

'And to be honest, I think I'm better at beating carpets than making them. So, yes, I'll make my arrangements to return.'

There were whoops and cheers all round and not just from the servants as by now a small crowd of mill workers had gathered round them too.

'We'll see you there, then, Sally.' Mrs Hartley smiled.

'And don't you be late,' Mrs Ackroyd added.

As the servants made their way out, James hung back. He was wearing his best blue checked shirt that Sally remembered from May Day and his nicely tailored brown trousers and braces.

'Might I have a word, Sal?' he asked. 'Would you come outside with me for a bit of fresh air?'

Sally felt utterly overwhelmed and her head was spinning all over again. She peeped at her father who gave her a tiny nod.

'Yes, James,' she answered eventually, as she picked up her shawl and hat before following him outside.

'Sal, I need to explain something,' James said as soon as they were through the shed door. The trees were beginning to turn golden and the leaves matched James's hair which was bathed in the early autumn sunlight.

'I never thought you capable of stealing anything, though I did a right bad job of making myself clear that day at Rushbearing.'

Sally opened her mouth to speak but James held his hand up.

'When you said that the Wheelers had been refused financial help from the master,' he continued, 'I was trying to explain that there's been some village gossip about Bertie.

'They say he's got a bit light-fingered, you know, to fund his drinking. They're also saying that his wife Freda's not ill at all and that she's actually made off for Scotland as it's all got too much for her now.'

'Then why did he want the vapour oil?' Sally asked.

'To sell,' James answered. 'It's quite valuable and he's desperate for money for his drink.

'I don't know whether there's any truth in it, but word reached Mr Julian and that's why he wouldn't help. I'm sure he'd have bought the oil for your ma, Sal. He knows you're genuine people.'

'I'm sorry I ran off without giving you a chance to explain, James,' Sally whispered, feeling her eyes fill with tears. 'I've cut off my hair for nothing.'

'You're as beautiful as ever, Sal,' James answered. His blue eyes were wide and full of intensity. 'You're so lovely, inside and out.'

Sally wasn't sure she was breathing any more. She was only aware of her thudding heart which felt ready to explode.

'Will you forgive me for being such a blinkered fool?' James went on. 'I was so caught up with the idea of Nancy that I couldn see that my true love was right by my side all along. I haven't slept since you left the Hall, Sal. Nothing is right without you.'

Sally gasped.

'Do you really mean that, James?'

'I do,' he murmured as he gently reached for her hand. 'Let's go home, Sally, Together.'

They turned back up the path towards the Hall and walked together in the gentle autumn breeze which sent fallen leaves swirling around them.

Sally smiled quietly to herself as she felt the warmth from James's hand, which was still entwined with hers, spread right to her soul.

It was just as she'd known all along; they were the perfect fit.